When Delilah Smiles

A touch as light as a feather
awakens the heart in a dark world.

When Delilah Smiles

by Sunnie Day

A touch
as light as a feather
awakens the heart
in a dark world

Laurus BOOKS

When Delilah Smiles

by Sunnie Day

Paperback Book: ISBN-13: 978-1-938526-12-1
E-Book: ISBN-13: 978-1-938526-13-8

Senior Copyeditor: Nancy E. Williams
Cover Designer: Jennifer Tipton Cappoen

Published by LAURUS BOOKS

Printed in the United States of America

LAURUS BOOKS
P. O. Box 894
Locust Grove, GA 30248 USA
www.TheLaurusCompany.com

Table of Contents

Acknowledgement

I would like to say a special thank you to my friend, Mike Friedman, who was an endless well of support as I began to write this story. He helped me edit the rough draft early on and pick out the picture of the feather. He continued to tell me that this was a story worth telling and encouraged me to publish. Thank you, Mike, for your friendship and support, as now *When Delilah Smiles* has come into the world to shine.

Chapter One

The Pregnancy

Adam looked out the window. The sky was dark, and lights flickered off the bay. It was March, and the weather was still cold and damp. He looked over at Kate sleeping soundly. She looked like an angel. He enjoyed early-morning conversations with her and usually tried to persuade her to get up with him when he was awake. This morning, he hesitated because she had been feeling tired and, frankly, a bit grumpy. Adam decided he would have to wake her this morning. He couldn't keep this to himself much longer. He had something he needed to ask her.

For the last few weeks, Adam had been looking for the perfect ring. It seemed nothing caught his eye. Katie was not a frills kind of woman and was highly conservative when it came to spending big bucks on material things. It might have been that she never had that much growing up. He knew the ring could not be flashy or too costly. He finally found a simple, half-carat diamond set in a white gold band.

Adam had played out the scenario in his mind many times as to how he would propose. Nothing seemed to fit. Katie was the most loving woman he had ever met, but she was not big on pomp and circumstance. Her idea of a good time was a picnic in the park or sitting at a Cal Bears football game wrapped up in a blanket drinking hot chocolate. It did not take much imagination to come up with a proposal.

Deciding that he could wait no longer, Adam made his way over to the bed and lay quietly beside her. He ran his fingers along the frame of her face, thinking what a lucky man he was. They had been together for 12 years today. He knew he had told her in the past that marriage was just a word, that they didn't need a piece of paper to keep them happy, and many other such foolish things. When it came down to it, Adam wanted her to be his wife. He loved her. Leaning closer, he whispered in her ear, "Katie, wake up, my sleeping beauty. I have something for you."

Sleepily, Katie opened her eyes to find Adam holding a beautiful diamond ring on his pinky finger.

"Happy anniversary, Katie! Will you marry me?" He hadn't meant to blurt it out in two short sentences. It must have been his nerves.

Kate sat up and looked at Adam with a surprised look on her face. "I can't believe you are asking me after all this time. I thought you didn't want to get married," Kate blurted out with a sleepy but perplexed look on her face.

Smiling, Adam wiggled the ring and said, "Please, say yes, Katie."

It had been ten years since Adam graduated from law school and Kate received her degree in journalism. They had met in college. Adam was attending law school, and they found one thing in common: both of them were older students. Kate was 32, and Adam was 39 years old. Life's challenges kept them from going to college when they were in their twenties, so they found themselves attending a university with much younger students.

One particular quarter, they both happened to sign up for the same business class. Kate had arrived early one day and looked up to see this guy coming toward her as if he were on a mission. Adam had long red hair tied back in a ponytail and a short beard. He stood about six feet tall, with a slim build.

"Excuse me. It seems as if you are in my seat," Adam said, smiling.

Kate was a petite woman with long brown hair and brown eyes. Adam, being a creature of habit, found himself without his original seat and standing over the prettiest woman he had seen in a long time. She looked up and said, Oh, does this seat have your name on it?" Adam didn't know what to say. He actually blushed and felt as if he were back in high school. Choosing not to make a scene, he took the seat behind her.

After class, Kate stood up and looked at Adam. "You can have the seat tomorrow, or maybe we can share," Kate said with a smile. Then she walked away. Adam knew at that moment they would be sharing more than a chair if he had his way.

Adam was from the San Francisco area and worked as a security guard for the city. His marriage, right out of high school, had lasted only six months before his young wife ran off with some guy she had met at a concert. Adam decided to go back to school. Funds were low, but he worked at night and attended school during the day. With such a marital history, Adam was definitely not looking for another wife. He had been hurt badly and was not ready to be hurt again.

Kate was another story. Her parents had died when she was four, and she and her brother Ben were placed in the foster care system. Kate's whole world had changed. Her brother Ben was eleven then. He joined the Army at seventeen, leaving her behind. He thought that if he joined the service, one day he could take care of his little sister. The Army had other plans, and mission after mission took him farther away from her. He wrote her many letters, but he could not get home as he had planned.

Their foster parents were older, but they gave Kate the love and care she needed. Around the time of her high school graduation, her foster dad had a stroke and died. Kate stayed to care for her foster mom, and the months turned into years. Kate woke up to reality one day and realized that she was a 32-year-old woman who needed to do something with her life. Her foster mother had just passed away, and Kate felt that she was finally free to leave. That was when she had enrolled in college.

The day after Kate and Adam first met, Adam made sure he was in class early. Deep down he was hoping to see the feisty young woman who had stolen his seat. He walked into the classroom to find her sitting in the seat behind his.

"I see we're sharing," Adam said, smiling at Kate.

"I believe you're right," said Kate, smiling back.

"Since we are sharing, I was wondering if you would like to go for coffee after class," Adam asked hopefully.

"Will we have to share a seat there, too?" Kate asked as she giggled.

"I think we can negotiate that, don't you?" Adam answered playfully.

After that coffee date, Adam and Kate were inseparable.

Much later, they wondered if fate had a hand in their meeting. Kate's older brother Ben came home on leave from the Army to meet this new man in his little sister's life. Imagine the surprise on both men's faces when they realized they were friends from high school. Ben and Adam were, in fact, close friends and had spoken often. Having no idea that the new woman in Adam's life was Ben's own little sister, this news came as a shock. Ben told Kate that there was not another man on earth whom he thought would be better for her than Adam. He loved Adam like a brother.

Kate was going to school to become a journalist and Adam to become a lawyer. They spent many days talking in the local coffee shops, walking in the nearby park, and holding hands in the library. Love was in the air, and nothing was going to stand in its way. Like a couple of young lovers, they relived the time they had lost in their twenties.

Once they graduated from Berkeley, the only decision they had to make was where they would live. They bought a quaint house in El Cerrito that overlooked the San Francisco Bay. It was quite charming, with two small bedrooms, a living room, one bath, a kitchen, a tiny eating area, and an attached garage. It had belonged to Mr. and Mrs. Dunphy who had lived there for sixty years. Mr. and Mrs. Dunphy's daughter Linda, who sold them the house, told them that her parents bought it for $5,000 back in the day. There was one large orange tree in the backyard that still produced delicious fruit.

Marriage was only for other people. Kate and Adam loved each other, but both were busy getting their careers off the ground. Kate took a job with the local newspaper and became one of their most valued reporters. Adam built his law firm from scratch. He started representing some patrons who could not afford to pay him. People would pay what they could afford, but Adam never seemed to worry. He enjoyed doing *pro bono* work. Kate often told him that he wouldn't get ahead if he continued giving generous free services. In reality, however, she loved his kind heart.

Now, after all these years, Adam had proposed, and Kate was faced with trying to make sense of this unexpected turn of events. Suddenly, Kate looked very peaked.

"Hold that thought, Adam. I think I'm going to be sick."

Kate jumped out of bed and ran to the bathroom. Adam ran after her and found her on her knees hugging the toilet bowl, vomiting.

"Katie, are you okay? What's wrong?" Adam asked, holding her hair back away from her face.

"I'm pregnant, Adam. That is what's wrong. I'm going to have a baby."

Adam sat down beside her and looked at her in shock.

"You can close your mouth now, Adam," she told him sarcastically, wiping her mouth with a washcloth.

"How? When? I mean how long have you known?"

"I just took a test last week and had planned on telling you this weekend."

Kate studied Adam's face. She could tell he was confused. His reaction was not the one she had thought she would see. She had played this scene repeatedly in her mind, but he was not playing his part.

"I have a doctor's appointment in two weeks, and I would like you to come with me. Adam? Do you hear me? I have an appointment."

"Oh, of course, I will be there. I'm just in shock. Wow, a baby."

Adam slowly pulled the ring from his pinky finger and

put it back in his pocket. Kate noticed but didn't say a word.

"Katie, I don't know what to say. This is such a shock."

"You already said that, Adam. Now help me up."

Kate got up, washed her hands and face, and rinsed her mouth. Adam was still standing there watching her every move.

"Kate, I think I'm going to take a walk. Would you like to go with me?"

"No, thank you. It's too cold and wet for me. You go ahead. I'm going back to bed," said Kate sadly.

Adam slipped on his boots and a heavy coat. Closing the door quietly behind him, he made his way to the park that overlooks the Golden Gate Bridge. He and Kate often sat there watching the sun go down. Adam had never before felt such turmoil. "Why can't I be happy about the news?" he questioned himself. His mind was flooded with thoughts, and he had to sort them out.

I am a 51-year-old man. A baby never entered my mind. I thought this would never happen. I am an educated man. I know the risks of having a baby at our age. I finally have my life together, and we're free to do what we want. I can't imagine having a child to tie us down. Oh, God, what if something were wrong with the baby? What would we do? I have never been a shallow man, but this scares me. How do I face Katie and tell her my fears? I know she won't understand. I don't understand my feelings myself. What is wrong with me? What kind of monster am I? Maybe I don't deserve to have Kate after all. She deserves someone who will love her through anything that may come her way.

Tears began to flow down Adam's face. He knew he had to be strong. *I will walk back into that house, stand beside Katie, and pretend to be happy, no matter what!* Adam knew he would have to put on the performance of his life.

Walking slowing back to the house, the rain began to fall, but it did not seem to faze Adam. The house was quiet as Adam tiptoed into the bedroom, not wanting to wake up Kate. Taking off his wet clothes, he climbed into the warm bed with Kate, placing his arms tightly around her. How he wished she would turn over and face him.

"Kate, are you asleep?"

Kate didn't answer.

Adam breathed a sigh of relief and fell asleep.

Kate lay there in silence, holding onto her pillow tightly as tears streamed down her face. This was not the reaction she had envisioned. Adam's embrace felt cold and hurtful.

Two weeks had passed since Kate gave Adam the news of the baby. Words were rare between them. She was not sure what he was thinking, and in turn, he had no idea what was going through her mind.

The alarm rang loudly in Kate's ear, and she hurried to the bathroom, since this had been the morning ritual for the last three weeks. She couldn't seem to keep anything down, and mornings were the worst.

"Are you okay in there?" Adam asked loudly through the door.

"Yes, just leave me alone!" She took a shower, brushed her teeth, and made her way back into the bedroom, feeling very weak and nauseated.

"Katie, can I get you anything?" asked Adam in an upbeat voice, smiling at her.

"It looks like it's going to rain today. Better dress warmly," Adam advised her.

Kate looked at him with a disgruntled face and contempt in her very soul. How dare he even try to act concerned! Collecting her anger, she said, "My appointment is at ten o'clock. We need to leave the house soon."

She felt his eyes looking at her as she pulled her sweater over her head. She pulled on some jeans and could tell they would be tight. Already her belly was feeling like it was swollen. After a couple of tries, she finally got them buttoned.

"Quit staring at me, Adam."

"I'm sorry. I didn't mean to. I just think you are … never mind."

"You think I am what?" Kate asked as she turned, giving him an evil glare. "A beautiful pregnant woman, and you are so happy I'm carrying your child? That this is the most amazing thing in the world? What, Adam? What were you going to say?"

Adam threw the remote on the bed and stormed out of

the room. Kate heard the door slam as he left the house. She wasn't sure if he would show up for the appointment or not, and right then, she couldn't have cared less.

She threw on her heavy coat, pulled the collar up around her neck, and put on her winter cap before heading for the car. Adam's car was gone, and an empty feeling started to form in the pit of her stomach. Have I pushed him too far?

Pulling up to the clinic, Kate saw two couples making their way inside. She had fifteen minutes until her appointment. She looked around for Adam's car, but it was nowhere in sight. She had a bad feeling that he might not come. Grabbing her purse, she headed into the clinic and sat among the happy couples. Some of the expectant mothers looked as if they were due any day. They looked so young. She knew she appeared much older, but, thankfully, she wasn't showing yet. One young mother sat beside her, and it was easy to tell she was due about any day. She smiled as she sat down.

"Hello, I'm Barb. How far along are you?"

"Just found out about three weeks ago. Think I'm about six weeks along," Kate said, attempting to smile.

"I was due last week. Looks like they will have to do a C-section on me."

Kate looked at Barb. She may have been all of eighteen. There was no ring on her finger. Barb picked up her backpack and pulled out a science book. It suddenly hit Kate that the girl was still in high school.

"Kate Moore," a nurse called from the front desk.

Kate smiled at Barb, whispered, "Good luck," and then hurried to the front desk, where she was escorted to the examining area to a clean, sterile room.

"The doctor will be with you in just a moment. Please undress and put on this hospital gown," the nurse said, walking quickly out the door.

Kate put on the gown, neatly folded her clothes, and sat on the table. She looked out the window and observed the very wet and cold day. She wondered if Adam was going to come. Part of her wanted him to be by her side, but the other part said to tell him to get lost.

Suddenly, the door opened and in walked a woman in a white coat. "Hello, Mrs. Moore. I'm Dr. Ryan. How are you today?"

"I'm fine," Kate answered quickly and rather quietly.

"There is a gentleman out there who is waiting to come in. He says his name is Adam. Should I let him come back?"

"Yes, that would be fine," Kate answered, reluctantly.

The doctor left the room and returned with Adam. He walked to the exam table and planted a kiss on Kate's cheek.

"I told you I would be here," he whispered.

Adam sat in the corner as the doctor did the initial exam. The doctor then turned to Adam and asked him to come and sit by the table to view the first ultrasound. There, in Kate's uterus, was the tiniest little nugget, not a nugget but more like a piece of rice. They looked at each other in awe.

Adam actually smiled and seemed a bit excited. Kate's anger was slowly fading.

"Kate, get dressed, and you two meet me over in my office. I would like to discuss some things with you. Everything looks fine. We just need to go over a few things."

Adam and Kate looked at each other and knew this was the decisive moment. Their fears would be discussed fully.

Kate got dressed, and they moved next door to a nice, comfortable office. Dr. Ryan came in and pulled up a chair next to them. "I have to be truthful, Kate. Yours is a high risk pregnancy because of your age. Let me reassure you. It is very common for a woman your age to have a healthy baby, but there are risks. It puts you at a high risk for the baby to be born with Down syndrome. Your health is also a concern. We have to make sure your blood pressure stays normal. If not, we may have to put you on bed rest. We may have to do a C-section should you not be able to deliver via a normal vaginal delivery, which sometimes happens with first-time pregnancies. There is also a risk of the baby being born prematurely, and we really want to keep this little one inside as long as we can."

Looking at Adam, the doctor continued, "That means Mom needs lots of rest, and Dad needs to help as much as he can."

Adam looked like a deer caught in the headlights. He didn't smile. He sat like a statue—rigid—appearing to be without feeling. He was staring at the doctor almost as if he had checked out.

"Are you okay, Adam?" the doctor asked.

"Uh-huh," answered Adam in a boyish tone.

The doctor then looked back at Kate and said, "If the baby were to be born prematurely, other problems could occur. I don't want to scare you, but since you have a high-risk pregnancy, there are always concerns."

Kate could see the doctor's lips moving but could no longer hear her words. The room began to appear smaller, and she slowly drifted off into her own world thinking about the day she took her pregnancy test.

Adam was at work. I was about a week and a half late, which is unusual for me, and I had been feeling tired. I went to the store and bought my very first pregnancy test kit. I kid you not. In all my years, I never missed a period. I placed the test on the counter, feeling like an underage kid buying cigarettes. It felt as if everyone in the world was watching. The young cashier looked at me with curiosity. She probably thought I was buying this for my daughter.

As soon as I got home, I took the test. It was the longest five minutes of my life. I watched the little blue line pop up and knew I was indeed pregnant. I was thrilled but scared, too. I had to tell Adam. He would be so excited. We were having a baby! I decided that I should wait for a couple more weeks, just to be sure, and then I would tell him.

"Kate," said the doctor, touching Kate's shoulder.

"Oh, I'm sorry, Doctor," Kate said, a little embarrassed, not knowing how much of the conversation she had missed.

"Your due date is November 8th. I will see you back in two weeks. We should be able to hear a heartbeat by then. Here is your prescription for your prenatal vitamins. If you have any problems, please call my office."

She shook their hands and wished them well. Adam and Kate left the doctor's office without a word and without meeting each other's eyes.

Lying there in bed, Kate did not open her eyes, although she had been awake for a while. Four months had passed, and she was beginning to show. The baby started to move a little inside. It felt like little butterflies in her stomach. She tried to get Adam to feel her belly, but he had no interest. He tried to be kind and offer small talk, but he did not touch her. They had not made love since he found out she was pregnant.

Kate's mind retraced events of the last few months.

The day we went to the doctor to hear the heartbeat for the first time, Adam was amazed at the ultrasound. To see a beating heart was truly miraculous. I have prayed every day that he would perk up and his heart would wrap around the idea of having this baby, but I'm afraid it's not happening. He truly has distanced himself from our baby and from me.

Sometimes I think he has only stayed out of guilt.

The last couple of days, Kate felt an uneasiness in her heart. It was an unsettling feeling. She finally opened her eyes to find Adam looking out the window. Then she saw his packed bags waiting by the door. She knew that what she feared most was coming true.

Seeing that she was awake, Adam walked over to the bed and sat down beside her. She had never seen him look so dejected. "I can't do this, Katie. I will help in any way I can. I will send money and pay the hospital bills, but I can't be a father. You'll be better off without me." Tears rolled down his face as he spoke.

Kate lay there numb. No tears would come. Adam bent over to kiss her forehead, but she turned her face away. Picking up his bags, he opened the door and walked away.

The little butterfly inside Kate's belly danced as if to say, "Don't be sad. We are going to be all right."

Adam walked to the car with his bags. The weight he was carrying inside was almost unbearable. His heart was heavy. He could hardly breathe. He sat down in the car and placed both hands on the steering wheel. He stared out the window and then dropped his head. His thoughts were berating him.

I have just walked out on the mother of my child while she's carrying my baby. What kind of man does such a thing? I will tell you what kind of man: a coward, a low down, good for nothing coward!

Adam started the car and drove out of the driveway of the home he had shared with Kate for over a decade. He loved her, but his sense of panic was overwhelming.

I can try to explain how I am feeling, but it would only sound like excuses. I have been pretending to be happy, and I can't deceive Kate for one more minute. She deserves better. A part of me thinks I would not make a good father. My pop left when I was five. I watched him pat me on the head and walk out the door. I never saw him again. What do I know about being a father? I never had one.

To think I could take care of a child who may have disabilities seems beyond my reach. I have trouble keeping a plant alive. I have barely been able to take care of myself. Kate has always been the one to take care of me. How does one know how to be a good father? What if being a father doesn't come naturally to me? I would only be prolonging a horrible situation. What if, in five years, I do the same thing my father did to me?

Adam was moving out of town, just far enough that he would not run into Kate. "That would tear my heart out," he had thought. "She has Beth and Eddie to step in and help. She doesn't need a loser like me."

He turned onto the highway toward his new home. *I thought leaving was going to be a relief, but if what I am feeling is any indication of the future, life for me is only going to spiral downward very fast. I can't help but think of Kate.*

Chapter Two

The Diagnosis

*A*dam had been gone for almost a year when Kate and Baby Delilah arrived for the doctor's appointment she had dreaded for so long.

The diagnosis was Retinitis Pigmentosa. They called it "RP," a disease that causes blindness in premature infants. Delilah's retinal blood vessels were not fully developed. The doctors could not yet tell what their degree of development was. The test done at birth detected the condition, but it had been a wait and see time as to the extent of her vision loss. Her hearing loss was also part of a congenital defect. They called it Usher Syndrome.

Kate could still hear the sternness in the specialist's voice as he delivered the news. "Your baby will never develop into a 'normal child.' She will most likely have several learning disabilities and be blind. And she won't hear the sound of your voice." His words were like sharp daggers going straight into Kate's heart.

~ KATE ~

How does one respond to this kind of news? I wanted to stand up and yell at him, "How dare you say that about my baby!"

I knew he was just doing his job. His clinical coolness disturbed me though. He showed no emotion and no thoughtfulness about the words he was speaking to me. Maybe he has had to deliver this kind of news so many times that he has lost his empathy and his caring touch. I couldn't imagine having to sit down and tell parents this news. It was hard enough being on the receiving end of this conversation.

"Do you have any questions for me, Ms. Moore?"

I looked at him blankly and said, "I don't believe so."

"Here is the phone number of someone who may be able to help you with Delilah. Her name is Mrs. Hamilton. I think she will be invaluable to you in the future. I hope you will call her." He nonchalantly handed me a tissue. We shook hands and said our goodbyes.

Just as I was leaving, the doctor turned around and touched my arm. I will never forget his words: "Kate, life has a way of giving us many challenges. Just remember that God never gives us more than we can bear."

I smiled slightly and nodded my head, believing that the God I knew would not let me down. His words were comforting, and I planted them deep within my heart.

At that moment, a thought came to me. *It is not about Delilah being blind and deaf. It is about me being able to give my precious baby all she needs.*

I wasn't sure how to take care of a baby with these kinds of needs. I worried that it wouldn't come naturally to me. *Will we bond as mother and child if she can't hear or see me? How does all of this work?* My mind was racing with all kinds of questions that I knew only time would be able to answer.

I looked down at my beautiful child with her soft, red curls peeking out from under her winter cap. "Delilah, my sweet baby, this doctor is only speculating about the possibilities." I was determined to believe in the impossible.

I opened the car door and pulled Delilah close as the cold wind blew, sending a chill through me. All I could think about was getting Delilah home. The cold air took my breath away, and my tears felt like frozen icicles on my cheeks. The snow began to fall, forming a soft blanket on the ground. I climbed into the car with tears flowing. I had no apologies for my raw emotions that had begun to spill out.

I prayed that the heater would warm up this old piece of metal fast as I started the car. I needed to collect my thoughts. I couldn't drive in this condition. With Delilah fast asleep, I sat there holding her close to my heart.

My car was facing an empty playground. I watched as snowflakes settled onto the swings, covering the seats until they had cushions of snow. I thought about God and how

He would hold us up. With each passing day, I would allow Him to be my swing, holding my every trial and worry. I had to believe this. I had nothing else to depend on.

My mind drifted back to the day I found out I was expecting a baby. I thought I would never be able to get pregnant. When I was younger, I had many female problems and ended up visiting one doctor after another. After being told repeatedly that I would probably never be able to conceive, I had given up on ever bearing a child.

It was also hard to get pregnant if you were not sexually active. I had not met anyone who had made me want to be intimate before I met Adam. I held some strong values about sex and marriage, which my foster mom had instilled in me. I dated a little, but I always seemed to sabotage myself and destroy any hope of getting serious. The thought of a happily-ever-after ending was something that happened to others, not me. After I lost my parents and then couldn't be around Ben, I felt abandoned. I didn't give my heart away easily. However, I had always thought that one day I would like to get married.

My relationships never lasted, until I met Adam. He was different. He was kind, and it appeared that he was the one. We were so good together. In the beginning, he never pushed me to be with him. He had a different view of marriage than I did. He felt that it was just a piece of paper. He always said he didn't need marriage to prove he loved me. I still dreamed of marrying him one day.

We had a healthy sex life, but there was one special night that I remember most of all. Adam had gone out of town for a convention for a week. We had never been apart for that long. It was the week before Valentine's Day. While he was gone, I planned a very romantic evening. I picked him up at the airport and didn't tell him where I was taking him until we were there. We checked into the hotel where I had made reservations. I had brought along our bags with changes of clothes. I was never one to get dressed up, but I wanted that night to be special. I had found the cutest black dress that opened in the back. He wore black dress pants and a light green cotton dress shirt that matched his eyes.

I had also made reservations for us to go on a chartered boat called the "Pacific Horn Blower." We had a window seat that gave us a beautiful view of the bay at night. Dinner was perfect. We nibbled on strawberries while we sipped champagne. Making our way upstairs, we danced under the moonlight. I knew without a doubt that Delilah was conceived in love that night.

About four weeks later, Adam and I celebrated twelve years together. In one doctor visit two weeks after that, our whole world shifted. I was forty-four at the time, which meant I was going to have a high-risk pregnancy. Adam changed after that. Granted, since he was fifty-one, I'm sure that he was scared, too.

He didn't seem to be at all excited about the pregnancy. Did he just not want children, or did he fear the possibility that our child might have medical problems? I tried so hard to get him engaged in the pregnancy. Many nights I would suggest possible names from the baby book of names, but he would just agree with whatever I suggested. He never had an opinion.

I was four months along when he told me that it was over and walked away. I didn't stop him. I didn't shed one tear. I knew that it would be only my baby with me facing an unknown future. The man whom I had known and loved was not the one who abandoned me. Sometimes I thought I pushed him away. I pushed him so hard that he couldn't do anything but leave. How could he ask me to marry him one minute and then walk out the door the next? God, please explain this one because I don't understand.

After Adam left, I spent the next few months concentrating on the baby. I tried to push thoughts of Adam far from my mind. My belly grew, and I felt life inside me. I didn't feel alone. Everyone at the office was great and forever fussing over me.

I began decorating the nursery, and that brought me much enjoyment. The room was gentle and inviting. It was decorated in lavender, and the crib was white. I placed it by the picture window that overlooked the bay. The lights at night cast a soft glow into the room. I placed a white rocker beside the crib. I couldn't wait to hold my baby in my arms. The birth couldn't come quickly enough for me.

When my water broke, I was at the newspaper. I had

stopped in to make the final arrangements for my working at home. It was the middle of September, and I wasn't due until November 8th. I had been having some problems with my blood pressure, and the doctor had put me on bed rest. My boss, Eddie, was fantastic. He was very understanding and had been throughout my pregnancy. He was such a good friend.

"Kate, are you okay? You look kind of pale."

Eddie looked down at the floor and started yelling, "Oh, my God, Kate's water has broken! Oh, my God, someone get on the phone and call 9-1-1!"

"Eddie," I yelled at him. "Eddie, stop! Just take me to the hospital."

"Oh, right, the car!"

Beth, a reporter, was usually the cool one. She started running around the office nervously getting my purse and helping me out the door. I had never seen her so frazzled. She was yelling at Eddie that the car was parked out front.

Eddie ran in from the back door. As he ran past us, he was yelling to Beth, "I got this, Beth. Just don't have a cow!"

Beth looked at me and said, "When the good Lord said, 'brains,' Eddie thought he said, 'trains,' and answered, 'No, thanks, I'm not going anywhere!' "

"Beth, please don't make me laugh. Remember, I'm having a baby here."

"Oh, honey, laugh now 'cause you will be cryin' later," Beth said, only about half giggling.

I don't know what I would have done without those two. Half of the time, they were going at it. Next, they were giving each other these little smiles and winks. They thought no one knew about their secret love, but it was quite obvious to everyone in such a small office.

Eddie drove while Beth tried to comfort me. "Darlin', now you breathe like this." Beth began to pooch her lips out, pushing air back and forth in a very dramatic way.

I caught Eddie looking at the rearview mirror, watching her bosom go up and down. A smile crossed his lips, and he said, "Now, that is a sight for sore eyes."

"My gosh, you two, give it a rest! Do you not know I'm having a baby here?"

"Eddie, you behave yourself," Beth said with a wink.

I tried to think of anything except the pain. And then all I could think about was Eddie and Beth.

The office gossip was that these two had been seeing each other, but you'd never know it. Theirs tended to be a love-hate relationship. Eddie was the editor in chief, and he could be hard-nosed and a bit callous at times. Beth, the head reporter, was sweet and sassy. She wouldn't take Eddie's bull. They made for colorful days.

Both were widowed and were in their early sixties. Eddie had taken over the paper after his father died. Beth had moved from Georgia after the death of her husband. She said that she had just wanted a change. From a small town in Georgia to San Francisco, I would say she made a big jump.

Beth had just shown up one day in a red dress and red high heels, with red lipstick and bleached-blond hair. Her cleavage was bursting forth, and every eye looked up when she walked in. Eddie called her into his office, and you could hear a pin drop. He looked up to discover all of his reporters looking up with their mouths open. Beth was truly a Marilyn Monroe.

Eddie yelled from his office, "What are you guys looking at? Get back to work!" Thirty minutes later, Beth came out with a big smile and blew kisses as she walked by on her way out the door. Eddie came out and made an announcement, "I want you to meet Beth Maples. She's our new reporter."

Beth turned around and faced all of us and said, "Nice to meet y'all. I look forward to working with y'all."

The rest of us knew better than to say anything, so we mumbled, "Welcome. Nice to have you," and continued the work in front of us.

The next day Beth came into the office bright and early, this time wearing a peach sundress, peach heels, and peach lipstick. And she looked like a million dollars.

That was five years ago, and we have worked closely together ever since. Looks can be deceiving because Beth may be flamboyant, but she has a heart bigger than Texas. Leave it to Beth, and she will find and report a story better than anyone else. She has a way with people and can get into places that we never could.

One more strong contraction and my mind snapped

back to the here and now. The contractions were coming fast and furiously. I had felt cramping off and on all day but had told myself that it was too early. Once again, I tried to think of something else. The pain eased, and my mind again drifted back to the past.

After Adam left, Beth would come over and sit with me for hours. With her thick Southern drawl, Beth always made me laugh. I still hear her telling me, "Now, darlin', you just hang in there. No man is worth those tears."

The stories she could tell about her family made the hair on my arms stand up. I didn't feel so bad about my life after hearing about her Cousin Boe, Aunt Franny, and Grandpa Willie.

Suddenly, Beth hit Eddie on the back of the head with her purse and yelled at him to hit the gas. "What was that for, Beth? I'm going as fast as I can," yelled Eddie.

"At this rate, I'm going to have to shave my legs again before you get there!" countered Beth.

We arrived at the hospital just in time to get me into the birthing room. The baby's head had started to crown. Dr. Ryan came in and squeezed my hand.

"Kate, are you ready to meet your daughter?" I smiled and then let out a shriek. She was ready to meet the world. It seemed like only minutes had passed when I finally heard her cry. It was music to my ears. Since she was premature by about eight weeks, they took her to recovery right away. I lay there feeling empty and scared, not knowing what the outcome would be. I just wanted to hold my daughter and count her fingers and toes. The nurses kept reassuring me about my little girl. They came and updated me on the hour.

Five hours had passed, and I was finally allowed to go to the nursery and hold her for the very first time. She had a tiny nasal cannula under her nose to help her breathe. She was wearing a small cap on her head and was wrapped tightly in a pink baby blanket. My angel was very tiny and appeared so fragile. She was beautiful.

I peeked under her cap and could see a head full of hair that had a red tint in the light. She had Adam's red hair. As tiny as she was, she still looked perfect and healthy. *Adam, you are missing the most wonderful miracle today—the birth of our daughter. I'm going to call her Delilah.*

Morning came, and Beth got up from the chair to look in the mirror. She said, "Oh, girl, I have to go home. I look a mess. You don't mind, do you, sweetie? I'll be back. I can't let those good-lookin' doctors see me like this. I have to put on some more lipstick. Okay, darlin', you're all right. Need anything?"

I gave her a hug. "Thank you, Beth, for being here for me. I don't know what I would have done without you."

"Oh, honey, it was my pleasure. I'll be back soon."

As promised, Beth and Eddie showed up again with a huge, pink teddy bear wearing a bow with pink polka dots.

"Sweetie, Eddie just had to get this for the baby," Beth said, smiling. "Of course I wanted to get her a gift certificate to the spa, but Eddie said that was a little much."

The hospital staff wanted to make sure my blood pressure was under control before discussing my discharge. I spent days in the nursery feeding and holding Delilah when they allowed me to do so. She was breathing well on her own, and she appeared to be getting stronger every day. The doctors began to do some testing and were concerned about her vision and hearing.

Beth stayed by my side until I was discharged. To pass the time, Beth amused me by painting my toenails and fingernails, and also fixing my hair. I had a new look every day. Part of me felt like I was her personal Barbie® doll. If there had been another way to dye my hair, she would have tried to talk me into it, I am sure.

When I was discharged from the hospital, it tore my heart out. I couldn't bear to leave Delilah behind. Beth picked me up and took me home. I showered, dressed, and headed right back to the hospital. Forgetting my own discomfort, I packed a suitcase, booked a hotel room across the street from the hospital, and was able to stay with Delilah all day and night. At that time, the doctors suspected a few problems but said it would be a wait-and-see kind of thing. I had always been an optimist, so I was not going to let negative talk get into my mind.

At four weeks, Delilah was finally able to come home. She was doing well. All of her vitals were stable, and she was eating quite well. Eddie and Beth drove me to the hospital to pick her up. I had never envisioned leaving the hospital with a baby by myself—I mean without a husband, my child's father. Delilah was wearing a beautiful little dress that drowned her tiny body. Beth had picked it out. It was a bright yellow dress with tons of lace, matching booties, a matching blanket, and a matching hat.

When we arrived back at my house, I opened the door to find a brightly decorated house with pink balloons hanging everywhere. Everyone from the office was there for our homecoming. I felt so blessed and grateful that I didn't have to be alone.

In the days after I brought Delilah home, it became clear that something was different about her. She was a quiet baby and appeared to be content. But during the next few weeks, she didn't seem to be able to focus on my face or to follow objects. She ate well. But she never seemed to get startled by the sound of the doorbell, a dog barking, or any other loud noises. My touch brought a smile. Holding her in my arms, I would stroke her lovely little head and sweet body. She nestled in my arms as I sang to her. I never dreamed that she couldn't hear one note. I rocked her in my arms until she fell asleep. I knew that eventually I would have to hear a diagnosis.

When the appointment arrived, it was somewhat like receiving a sentence. As long as I had not heard those words aloud, Delilah and I could continue to live in our own make-believe little world.

The car had finally warmed up, and I felt as if I could drive home. With a sweet kiss planted on her cheek, I placed Delilah in her car seat and began our journey home.

Since I was still on maternity leave from my job for the next month, it would give me time to figure out what we had to do. As a writer, I was thankful that I would be able to work from home if I needed to. I glanced back and saw that my little one was awake and that she was staring out the window. I wondered to myself what she was seeing. Could she see colors and movements? Delilah was born almost two months early and weighed three and a half pounds. Looking at her now, I never would have guessed that she had been premature at birth. Her weight that day had even surprised the doctors. She appeared healthy in every way.

With her little fingers in her mouth, she sucked them in total contentment. No matter what the future held, we would handle it together. I watched in the rearview mirror as Delilah smiled. I wondered what she was smiling about. It always warmed my heart when I saw Delilah smile.

Chapter Three

The Intervener

~ KATE ~

I had honestly put off making the appointment for Delilah's follow-up, only because I didn't want to hear what the doctors had to say. But I knew I could no longer deny what I had observed.

The nurse gave me a pile of instructions on how to care for Delilah, but like anything, it always looks easier on paper. She also gave me a business card for a Mrs. Hamilton, a lady who specializes in services for the deaf and blind. The nurse explained that even though they didn't know the extent of Delilah's disabilities, it would be a good idea to talk with someone who could offer support.

Delilah had turned six months old, and the diagnosis had finally been confirmed: she is blind and deaf. I recall the nurse telling me that the earlier Delilah received help, the sooner she could adapt to the world around her. Maybe

I had thought I was all she would ever need. For six months, I tried to do it all. From what the nurse said, I realized that creating my own way of teaching Delilah may not be enough. For Delilah's sake, I needed help, and it was time to ask for it.

When we got home, I could feel my stomach growling and realized we both were likely hungry. I placed Delilah in her highchair and tucked a blanket around her for support and to make her feel secure. I opened a jar of chicken and dumplings, Delilah's favorite. When I placed the spoon to her lips, her arms started flailing in the air with delight.

Delilah never opens her mouth before the spoon touches her lips. Sometimes, when I don't feed her quickly enough, she will let out a big squeal and pound her hands on the highchair tray.

She always stares past me, and our eyes never meet. Her eyes are the most beautiful green, and at times, they have specks of brown. Her hair is curly and bright red.

When I finished feeding her, I leaned in to her ear and gave her a little kiss. She knew that this was the cue to get her out of the highchair, or that I was picking her up. She squealed with delight, since she knew a change was coming.

It was bath time, and I began our regular routine. I placed the bath soap near Delilah's nose, and her head turned in the direction of the soap. I got a small glass of water and placed her fingers in it. At first, during bath time, Delilah would cry so hard. I'm sure she didn't know what was going on. I learned that giving her a cue for what was going to happen next seemed to make bath time much easier. It took almost a month of doing this every day. I will never forget the day when Delilah's feet began to kick hard and a big grin came to her face when I gave her the cue. It was the first time she didn't cry during her bath.

After I gave Delilah her bath, it was time for our nightly dance. I played one of my favorite lullabies on the record player. The music danced around us as we swayed gently to the rhythm.

"Listen to the song he sings.
Can't you see the music brings her crystal sleep,
As her heavy eyelids fall, taking her to where
    the dolls rule the world,
And in the land of make-believe is where
    he leaves her sleeping,
Softly warm, in a crystal lullaby."

As we danced, the moon cast a soft glow through the window. I felt as if the lights from the bay were guarding Delilah and me through the night. I knew deep inside that she didn't hear the music, but she could feel the simple rhythm of the dance. She slowly laid her head on my shoulder, and I could feel her little body relax in my arms as she drifted off to sleep.

I have to face the reality of Delilah's world. It's no

longer about how I feel. It's about what Delilah needs.

I kissed her sweet cheeks and whispered, "Good night, my love," and placed her in her bed. I walked down the stairs, picked up the phone, and left a message for Mrs. Hamilton.

The last six months of caring for Delilah had been challenging, but with Delilah being my first child, it was all I knew. The nurse had said that she was putting in a referral for special services for me. I intended to contact them, but time had just slipped away.

Talking to Delilah's doctor earlier that day made me realize there was a whole world out there that I had not explored concerning deaf and blind children. I would have to learn sign language, since this would be the way Delilah would communicate for the rest of her life. I hoped Mrs. Hamilton would call me the next day. I was ready to do all I could to help Delilah have the life she deserved.

I went to my desk that was covered with books, publications, and articles about deaf and blind children and sat down.

In the beginning, I was like a sponge trying to take in every bit of information that I could find. I realized that I had only scratched the surface. I was already implementing some of the ideas into our daily routine. It was almost too overwhelming to try so much too quickly. However, in the back of my mind, I honestly didn't let it sink in that Delilah would be this way for the rest of her life.

Luckily, I made the decision early on that I would

concentrate on what she could do, not on what she could not do. I hoped that I had not let Delilah down and that Mrs. Hamilton would be pleased at what we had accomplished thus far. Delilah would be crawling soon and then becoming a toddler. I knew I needed all the help I could get.

My desk also had on it unfinished articles that I had to have done by certain deadlines for my job. Eddie, my boss, was so good to me. At night after Delilah was asleep was when I got the most done. Once again, I attempted to finish an article, since it was due in the morning. I thought about the unimportance of the new fall fashions, and I couldn't have cared less about the trends that were being set. I should have handed this article to Beth. I typed the last few paragraphs of the article and then hit send. Breathing a sigh of relief, I was glad to know that the article was finished and on its way to print.

Sleepily, I crawled into bed. The clock beside my bed read one o'clock. In only a few hours, I would be doing this all over again, alone. Sometimes I dreamed about Adam, and I got so angry with myself for still having feelings for him. No one understood that he had never been anything but good to me until the day he left. Something about this whole situation did not fit. How I wished that he had talked it through with me instead of letting it build up inside and walking away.

Mornings always came extremely fast. I hardly looked at the clock anymore to see exactly how much sleep I had the night before. It wouldn't change anything. A single mom with a special-needs child will always be chasing sleep. That is just a fact.

I walked into Delilah's room. She was lying in her crib, kicking her little legs and making her morning sounds. They were a little different in the morning, more high-pitched with an energetic ring to them. I leaned over and kissed her ear. She instantly started to squeal in delight. She knew it was her mama and that I was near. Her arms began to flap up and down, and her little smile was priceless. I picked her up and held her close. She touched my hair as if to reassure herself that it was indeed me.

I stroked her cheeks, reached down, and patted her bottom gently. This was our cue that I was going to change her diaper. She just now realized that when I pat her bottom and lay her down, a diaper change is coming. For a long while, she would let out a bloodcurdling scream until I picked her up again. I handed her a wipe, and she played with it in her hands. I gently stroked her legs with the cloth and then unfastened her diaper. Everything else went smoothly.

I realized early on that everything I did must have a physical cue. If she knew what was going to happen, then she was a lot happier and more secure. I got Delilah dressed in a green and white dress with tights. Her curly red hair stood out against that forest green color.

We headed downstairs for breakfast. I placed her in the highchair and propped a blanket around her little body.

While I prepared her oatmeal, I gave her a toy—a caterpillar that vibrates and sings. While she may not hear the music, the vibrations delighted her in every way. I watched as she brought it up to her lips, her cheeks, and even the top of her head.

Just as I was about to feed Delilah, the phone rang. It was Mrs. Hamilton. She had time that morning to come by and do an assessment. I was thrilled, thanked her, and hung up the phone. Then I began to have horrible butterflies in my stomach. *I hope I have not done anything wrong thus far. Have I done enough?* All of these thoughts flooded my mind. After feeding Delilah breakfast, I handed her a small washcloth, and she began to play with it. This was also one of our cues that I would be wiping the oatmeal from her face. I leaned in to give her a sweet kiss on her ear, letting her know that I would be picking her up.

We continued our normal routine, which was laying a blanket on the floor and playing with various toys. I helped Delilah attempt to sit up. She was almost there but still not quite ready. I gave her toys with different shapes. Her favorites were the ones that vibrated or were cold to the touch. She liked her teething rings, and of course, they went straight into her mouth.

Our favorite game was the airplane game. I kissed her ear so that she would know I was going to pick her up. I lay flat on my back, placed her facedown with her abdomen on my feet, held her hands in mine, and we went up and down.

I listened as she giggled out loud. When I stopped, she would stiffen up so rigidly that it was almost comical. It was her way of saying, "Let's do it again, Mama." Just as we were going for our fifth plane ride, the doorbell rang. I kissed Delilah's ear quickly and placed her back on the blanket. Smoothing my hair down and catching my breath, I answered the door.

"Hello, please come in. You must be Mrs. Hamilton," I said nervously.

"Hello, my dear. Yes, and you are Kate. And this must be Delilah," said Mrs. Hamilton, as she made her way to Delilah. "Oh, Kate, what a beautiful little girl you have here," said Mrs. Hamilton thoughtfully.

"Thank you. Yes, she is the love of my life."

I watched as Mrs. Hamilton pulled a big red heart on a long piece of leather from her purse and placed it around her neck.

"Dear, this is going to be my cue so that Delilah will know who I am when I come to visit. It will take a while, but she will soon know who I am just by touch," Mrs. Hamilton explained.

I felt the need to explain that I had read about cues and was using some of my own. She listened patiently as I told her what I had been doing and the cues that I had already been using. She seemed pleasantly surprised and happy.

Mrs. Hamilton, who was at least 60 years old, had over thirty years of experience in this field. She had raised two boys with their own challenges, both being deaf and blind. It was late in life when she had decided to help others. She was a family specialist, also known as an *intervener*. She and I would devise a plan and start a process that would follow Delilah until she reached school age and maybe even longer.

One of the first things that Mrs. Hamilton explained to me was profound. Many of the things that would affect Delilah would be influenced by the interactions Delilah had with me. My job was to help Delilah make sense of the world around her. Once the communication was established, a completely new world would open up for Delilah. Right now, it is just her and me. We have been in this safe cocoon. Even though she is only a six-month-old baby, Mrs. Hamilton said that we could start right away since time was on our side.

I explained to Mrs. Hamilton that Delilah seemed to use sensory touch mostly. She said that this was quite common in deaf and blind children, since that is how they learn within their environment. Mrs. Hamilton continued to explain that when Delilah touched objects with different textures, vibrations, and other stimulating activities, it would stimulate her curiosity.

Now it was time for Delilah to meet Mrs. Hamilton. I watched as this precious woman kicked off her shoes and leaned into Delilah's space. It was amazing to be an onlooker. Delilah began to stiffen up, and her little pouty lip came out. She knew instinctively that this was not me. Mrs. Hamilton was gentle and placed Delilah's hands around the large heart. Delilah quickly jerked her hands back and began to cry. Mrs. Hamilton got up and said, "Okay, my dear. This was a great first meeting. I shall see you tomorrow if that is good for you?"

I smiled and agreed to meet tomorrow. I realized at that moment that not only did Delilah need Mrs. Hamilton, but I also needed Mrs. Hamilton as a friend.

The day passed quickly, and I could hardly wait until Mrs. Hamilton returned. I felt as if she were there not only for Delilah but for me as well. I hadn't realized how lonely and isolated I had become.

Morning came, and I seemed to have more energy, more pep in my step, all because I felt hope once again. I sang and danced around the living room with Delilah in my arms like a little child, "Delilah, Mrs. Hamilton is coming for a visit today!"

After our little dance, I placed Delilah in her highchair for breakfast. She gave a little whimper because she wanted me to continue dancing.

The doorbell rang, and as promised, Mrs. Hamilton was right on time. "I hope I'm not too early," Mrs. Hamilton said as she smiled.

"Oh, no, please come in. Delilah is just getting ready to have breakfast."

"Perfect, it will give me a chance to observe her," Mrs. Hamilton explained.

Mrs. Hamilton followed me into the kitchen where

Delilah sat, pounding her little hands on the top of the high-chair tray. Mrs. Hamilton reached into her bag, pulled out the red heart, and placed it around her neck. She pulled up a chair next to Delilah, took her tiny hands, and wrapped them around the heart. This time Delilah stopped fidgeting and sat very quietly. Her eyes opened wider, and a slight smile formed on her little lips. Without warning, Delilah let out a big scream that startled even Mrs. Hamilton. There were no tears.

"Well, good morning to you, too, Miss Delilah," exclaimed Mrs. Hamilton, laughing loudly. Mrs. Hamilton watched as I touched Delilah's cheek softly and then touched her mouth with the spoon. Delilah gladly opened her mouth.

"Delilah is a happy baby, Kate. You have done well," said Mrs. Hamilton sweetly.

"Thank you, Mrs. Hamilton. I hoped you would think so." Tears began to form in my eyes. *Oh, how I needed to hear those words.*

"I'm sorry, Mrs. Hamilton. Please forgive my manners. May I offer you some coffee or tea?" I asked.

"Tea would be wonderful if it's not too much trouble," Mrs. Hamilton replied. "I will sit here with Miss Delilah and keep her company."

While preparing the tea, I peeked in on Delilah and Mrs. Hamilton. Mrs. Hamilton was leaning over the highchair with her rather sizable bosoms resting on the tray placing the red heart once more in Delilah's hands. Mrs. Hamilton was singing a song I hadn't heard before. She stroked Delilah's little hands as she held the heart tightly.

Over in Killarney
Many years ago,
Me mother sang a song to me
In tones so sweet and low.
Just a simple little ditty,
In her good old Irish way,
And I'd give the world if she could sing
That song to me this day.

Too-ra-loo-ra-loo-ral. Too-ra-loo-ra-li.
Too-ra-loo-ra-loo-ral. Hush now; don't you cry!
Too-ra-loo-ra-loo-ral. Too-ra-loo-ra-li.
Too-ra-loo-ra-loo-ral. That's an Irish lullaby.

I returned with the tea and sat beside Mrs. Hamilton.

"There are many things to learn, my dear, and it will take a lot of time. You will see, Kate, that life is going to be challenging, but it also will be rewarding. Delilah's world will become your world and your norm."

I never thought about it that way. *Her norm would become my norm*, I thought to myself.

"Kate, it will be you who will adjust to her world. She's already in it, living the best she can with what she knows. Everything is going to be like Christmas to Delilah. As you give her the tools she needs, you will be opening new doors into a world that she has neither seen nor heard. Our goal is that one day she will be independent and living with minimal assistance," explained Mrs. Hamilton with a smile.

Mrs. Hamilton's words changed my world in an instant.

"Each activity has to have a clear beginning and a clear ending. Her hands will be her means of communication. Her body will give you many cues as to how she is feeling. One thing I would like to start right away is sign language, Kate."

I would not dispute Mrs. Hamilton since she was the expert, but Delilah is only six months old. She would be seven months in a few days. *She is still a baby*, I thought to myself.

Mrs. Hamilton could tell that I was not totally on board with this idea and began to explain. "The most important gift we can give Delilah is a way for her to communicate with us and for us to communicate with her. There are many different ways to sign. For a baby, my favorite is body signing. It will take a very long time and lots of patience, but once Delilah has a way to communicate, her world will open up to her. She's the perfect age to start. You are already using many body signs and don't realize it. It is stress free and natural. The communication is instant. As she gets older, we will add other ways to communicate. This is a great place to start."

The day went by fast as Mrs. Hamilton and I watched Delilah play on the floor. We observed her at mealtime and when it was time to put her down for a nap. Then we sat down and devised a plan that would help Delilah and me move forward. Mrs. Hamilton will come three times per week in the mornings and work with both of us. As Delilah gets older, Mrs. Hamilton will work with her one-on-one every day. There is a school for the deaf and blind in the city where Delilah will be able to attend when she turns three. There is much to do, but now I feel as if there is a direction and there is hope for our future.

"Kate, dear, there is always hope that Delilah has some residual hearing. If she does, it would give her the opportunity to hear slightly with cochlear implants in the future. Only time will tell. For now, let's concentrate on the everyday tasks. Kate, I do want to say that even though Delilah is a baby, learning the finger signs, tactile signing, and other techniques will only help you to reinforce what Delilah will learn later," said Mrs. Hamilton.

I knew she was right. I had to be proactive and learn everything I could. I needed be able to help my daughter, and communication is the most important thing.

"Mrs. Hamilton, I have one more concern, and this is difficult for me to talk about. The doctor told me that Delilah might have some learning disabilities as well. What if she is not able to learn?" I asked nervously.

"My dear, if I had a nickel for every time a doctor or a teacher told me what my children could not do, I would be rich. You put that out of your mind, dear. We're going to concentrate on all that Delilah *can* do. Then we'll go from there," said Mrs. Hamilton with a reassuring smile.

Mrs. Hamilton was a boisterous-sounding woman, but as soon as her face turned toward Delilah, her tone was as sweet as honey. You could tell she loved her job.

She was slightly heavyset and wore a long gray skirt with a plaid blouse. Her shoes were black flats. Her long silver hair was pulled back in a ponytail that reached her waist and had a big purple bow attached. I noticed that on her blouse was a big, yellow, fragrant flower. I could smell the sweet fragrance from the time she walked in. I finally found the nerve to ask her why she always wore a flower, since I noticed that she had worn one during our last visit.

"Mrs. Hamilton, I love your flower. It smells so nice. If you don't mind me asking, is there significance behind the flower?" I asked her shyly.

"Well, aren't you the observant one, Miss Kate," Mrs. Hamilton said giggling. "There actually is a very good reason behind this flower that is attached to my, uh, rather large bosoms. It's a reminder to always stop and smell the flowers. You know, they are such gifts, Kate. Flowers are only around for a season, so we should admire them, love them, and respect them for the time they're here. Enjoy and admire them, I always say, sort of like our Delilah, here."

If possible, I had just fallen in love with our precious Mrs. Hamilton.

Days have turned into weeks and weeks into months since my call to Mrs. Hamilton. We have grown to be close friends, and Delilah learns more every day.

The last four months have been life changing for Delilah and me. With Mrs. Hamilton's help, we have managed to make a routine, set some goals, and implement them. Once a week, we meet with other families and share our progress and concerns. I've learned a lot from the support groups, and I don't feel so alone. So many changes have taken place that my head is reeling, but they have been good changes.

Mrs. Hamilton believes that Delilah might have very few developmental delays because she has been like a sponge up to this point. She has been learning new things every day. We found that she loves to keep busy. As long as she is busy, she is a happy baby.

The first thing that Mrs. Hamilton and I worked on was making our home a place where Delilah could thrive. Her environment needs to be user-friendly. As she grows, everything needs to have its own place, so she can explore and be safe as well. The living room became her play area. I removed my glass tables and ornamental glass pretties to enable her to move around without the fear of getting hurt.

She has started to crawl, and I wear my running shoes to keep up with her fast pace. At first, I worried about her hitting her head on the wall or on some other object. But Delilah has proven to have one hard head! I can't tell you the number of times I have heard a bonk sound and have come running to find her just sitting there. She would look dazed, as if she didn't know what had just happened. After she sat there contemplating, it wouldn't be long before she was off again on a new adventure.

She doesn't cry much when she gets hurt. She has such determination and drive. Mrs. Hamilton has held me back many times when I dropped everything to run to Delilah's aid. She would hold my arm. "No, Kate. Let her be," she would say. Over time, I understood the importance of Delilah learning on her own and making sense of the environment around her.

I bought some large, brightly-colored beanbag chairs. We were still unsure if Delilah could see any light, but there was a small chance that she could see a faint ray of light, which would be an amazing blessing.

We set up three stations, one in each corner of the room. In one station, toys that vibrated, balls, and shapes of all kinds were in a basket. There was also a small children's table with a chair.

In the second station, there was a rocking horse and Delilah's swing. She loved motion and had no fear of swinging back and forth or of rocking on the horse. Maybe she liked these because I had always danced with her before bed since she was born. I still had to assist her to get on the horse or into the swing. I watched as she would crawl to find them, as if she were on a mission. Once she reached her destination, she would bang her hands on the horse's head and make a noise specific to this station. I laughed to myself and called it her "cattle call." It sounded like, "Ahhh, oop, oop, ahhh." It was one of her favorite things to do.

In the third station was a box filled with many different-textured blocks and items that she could feel. I used blocks of wood and glued something with texture onto each of them—furry cloth, rough sandpaper, plastic, corduroy, velvet, corrugated cardboard, crinkled aluminum foil, rickrack, and many other textured items that she could feel. She spent a lot of time playing with the items in this box.

I have been amazed at how Delilah crawls to each corner and grabs different items to amuse herself.

Delilah loves walks to the park, so we added an outing to her daily routine, unless it's storming outside or the temperature is below zero. Mrs. Hamilton brought a small piece of chain, and Delilah learned that the chain is her cue for going outside. The swing at the park has a booster seat. I would put her in the seat and place her hands on the swing's chains. At almost one year old, she knew that the chain represented the swing at the park. Whenever she feels the chain, she knows that we are going outside to the park. Her little legs start swinging, and she displays that beautiful smile.

We have been working on other tasks as well, and I have seen many changes taking place. Delilah has learned how to drink from a cup, so I added a cup at each station. She will find the cup, hold it in her hand, and bounce up and down on her bottom while making a high-pitched noise that lets me know she wants a drink. If I have left the room, I can always tell when she has the cup in her hand. She would be drinking on the hour if it were up to her.

My days have been filled with taking care of Delilah. I have continued to work for the paper at night after she has gone to bed. In the beginning, Delilah rarely woke up, but she has started teething, and I don't get any work done some nights. Mrs. Hamilton thinks I should leave Delilah for one day a week, so I can have a break to avoid burnout. I haven't been able to bring myself to do that quite yet. There is a program in the city at the school for deaf and blind students that offers such a weekly respite. It is free, so I have decided I will look into it soon.

Today is Delilah's first birthday, and I invited many friends over from the center. Mrs. Hamilton is bringing the cake, and my brother Ben, whom I have not seen in over a year, is coming. Ben and I have always been close, but it was not until about three months before Delilah's birthday that I finally broke down and told him about Delilah. He is seven years older than I and has always felt like he needed to take care of me. He has been working overseas, and I didn't want him to drop everything to run to my aid. He had just gotten married, and they were living in Japan. He said he had a surprise for me, so I thought I was going to get to meet my new sister-in-law for the first time.

I remember calling him, crying, and telling him the whole story about Delilah. He couldn't believe that I had been handling everything all on my own. I could tell by his voice that he was really hurt that I hadn't shared with him about Delilah before now. I also could tell that if he could have gotten hold of Adam, there would have been some harsh words exchanged.

I had not had time to think about Adam, but today he was on my mind. He had always been such a gentle soul. I wondered if he ever thought about me or felt any remorse for walking out on me the way he did after learning about the possible complications of my high-risk pregnancy. Adam called a couple of times after Delilah was born, but I didn't take his calls. I was still too angry then, but not so much now. Deep down, I thought he would love Delilah, but I wasn't sure that I would ever know.

The party was due to start soon. I had decorated the house in bright pink and white balloons. Streamers hung from every corner. It was a Strawberry Shortcake® birthday. I think the party was more for me than for Delilah—the party that every little girl dreams of having. I dressed Delilah in a pink frilly dress, lacy socks, and black patent-leather shoes. The hat that looked so cute on her was a constant struggle because she took it off and into her mouth it went. I threw on some jeans and a plain pink top, twisted my hair up in a bun, and stopped for the day. My days of applying makeup, shopping for clothes, or finding that perfect outfit for just such an occasion had taken a backseat. I had about 30 minutes before everyone would arrive when the phone rang.

"Hello. Adam? I'm surprised to hear from you! I don't think today is a good day. Tomorrow? I guess so. We can meet tomorrow. Yes, we're still at the same address. Two o'clock is good. Okay. Bye."

The last thing I expected today was to hear from Delilah's daddy. I sat down holding Delilah close. "You have your daddy's red hair."

Chapter Four
Adam's Vision

~ ADAM ~

I *could hear her, but I couldn't find her. "Daddy! Daddy!" I tried to call out to her, but no words would come. Suddenly, there was silence. I saw her standing in a field of grass up to her waist. She was motioning for me to come to her, but there was no sound. I started walking toward her, but in an instant, everything turned black. I found myself in total darkness. Fear gripped me, and I stood motionless. I didn't know which way to go.*

I awoke in a cold sweat. This was the same dream I've had repeatedly for the last few months. *Oh, God, I don't know what this dream means.*

I walked to the bathroom and realized that tears were streaming from my eyes. My heart was pounding. All I could think about was Kate and the baby. *What kind of man walks away from his responsibility? I am such a coward.*

Panic had overcome me in the doctor's office hearing that we had a good chance of having a baby with disabilities. There could be no guarantees that our baby would be healthy because of our ages, and Kate's would be a high-risk pregnancy. It was more than I could bear.

I honestly had believed we would never have a child. We thought Kate was past her childbearing years. Everything was good the way it was. The pregnancy was such a shock to both of us. *It all took a bad turn, and I have to move beyond it.*

I looked in the mirror and saw a middle-aged man—a father who had a child he had never met. I remember well the night I told Kate I couldn't do this. I was trembling. She didn't cry, get angry, or say anything. She just turned away. I felt my heart breaking. I wanted to talk to her about my fears, but I had crossed the line. There was no going back. She knew exactly how I felt.

I wonder what our baby looks like. Does the baby look like Kate or me?

My mom would turn over in her grave if she knew what I had done—the same thing my old man did. He walked out on my mom and me when I was five. I watched the pain and struggle a single mom goes through. Maybe I had turned into my old man after all.

Do I even know how to be a father? I asked myself that same question over and over in my mind. *Is that why it was so easy for me to pick up and leave?*

I am ashamed to face Ben again. I wouldn't be surprised if he punched me in the face. He stopped returning my calls, so I'm sure he found out that Kate and I had split up. He's so protective of her. When he first found out we were dating, he was shocked but happy. He gave us his blessing and made me promise I would never hurt her. I made that promise without any reservations. Ben is the closest thing to a brother that I've ever had. I wonder if Kate told him the reason behind our breakup. So many loose ends needed resolution.

The clock read five o'clock in the morning. I would meet my child today for the first time. I didn't even know if it was a boy or a girl. I knew nothing about the baby I had helped to create, except that it was about a year old.

I spent the morning looking at old photos of Kate. I knew in my heart that I still loved her. The palms of my hands kept sweating. I had never stopped loving her. I picked up a picture, and a flood of memories poured out. It was one of our first camping trips up north. She was attempting to put up the tent. She was wearing a yellow halter-top, shorts, and a red bandana. She got mad at me because I kept snapping pictures instead of helping her put up the tent. After some time, I laid the camera down and tried to assist her, but we ended up wrestling and making love on top of the tent that was still lying on the ground.

It was almost time for me to leave for Katie's home. I showered, trimmed my beard, and put on some jeans and a white pullover shirt. How should one dress to see the woman he loves and the child he has never met?

Resting on the dresser was a little brown bear I bought a couple of months after I left. I wasn't really sure why I bought it. I had been watching a couple with their baby in a store. They seemed so happy. I caught myself following them around the store and hoped they wouldn't think I was a stalker. I wanted to see how this little family acted together. I pretended in my mind that they could be Kate and me. I saw the baby giggle with delight when they picked up a little brown bear. I couldn't help but smile, too. I looked at basketballs, thinking that I may have a son. When they left, I went over and picked up a bear, too. I thought that maybe one day I would be able to give it to my baby. When I paid for it, the cashier commented, "Oh, some little one is going to be happy tonight!" I put on a fake smile and nodded to her in agreement.

When I got home, I placed the little brown bear on top of my dresser, and that is where it had remained until now. It almost seems lame now that I think about it. *How can a little bear make up for my abandoning Kate and our baby?* Maybe I should leave it in the car.

I had moved a couple of towns away when we broke up because I couldn't stand the thought of running into Kate and the baby. I rented a small apartment and became absorbed in my work. I tried to call Katie a couple of times, but she never returned my calls. Who could blame her? I wanted so badly to explain myself, but all the excuses in the world wouldn't make the situation right. I wasn't sure why Kate had now agreed to see me.

Pulling up to Kate's house, I could feel my whole body shaking. I felt nauseated. I had no idea what to expect. After sitting in the car for at least fifteen minutes, I finally mustered up the courage to get out. Nothing Kate could do would make me feel any worse than I already felt. I tucked the bear under my arm, walked to the door, and rang the bell. I looked at my watch, and it was exactly two o'clock. The door opened and there stood Kate, as beautiful as ever. Her brown hair was pulled back in a ponytail. She appeared thinner, but Kate had always been petite. I smiled and started to hug her, but she jumped back. Why would I even try such a thing?

"Hello, Adam," Kate said coldly.

"Hello, Kate," I said cautiously. A pins-and-needles feeling suddenly swept over me. "Thank you for seeing me."

"Come in," Kate said and moved to the side as I entered the house. It was awkward. I wondered at that moment if I had made a big mistake by coming here.

I held out the bear like some kind of peace offering. Kate took it without a trace of a smile and quickly put it on the table.

"Delilah is asleep but should be awake soon if you want to sit down," Kate explained.

I continued standing, almost as if frozen in place.

"Delilah? A little girl?" Instantly, I felt a lump in my throat. Tears began to form in my eyes, and it took all of my strength to keep it together.

"Yes, Adam, our baby is a beautiful little girl. You happened to call on her birthday yesterday. She turned one year old." Crossing her arms and looking up at me slightly, Kate said, "She has your red hair, Adam."

"Really? She has my red hair? I would have thought she'd have your brown hair." *What a stupid thing to say!* I'm not sure what my reasoning was, maybe just to throw words in the air.

It was at that moment that I was prepared to explain it all. I opened my mouth to speak. "Kate, I was such a ..."

Kate looked me dead in the eyes. "Stop right there, Adam. I really can't go there. There are things you don't know. Before you say anything, I need to explain some things about Delilah."

"Is she okay? I mean, is she healthy?" I asked. As soon as those words came out of my mouth, I knew they were not the right words to have used.

"Yes, she is very healthy!" Kate retorted back sharply. "There are some things you need to know about Delilah. Once you hear what I have to say, you may decide to turn around and walk right out that door once again. Adam, there is no easy way to say this. Delilah is deaf and blind."

I suddenly felt sick to my stomach. Oh, God, I wanted to throw up. I didn't want to feel this way. *Get a grip, Adam.*

I sat down hard in the chair. "I don't know what to say, Kate. I didn't know. I'm so sorry."

Kate looked at me with fire in her eyes. I knew she was going to let me have it. And she had every right to do so.

"Adam, there's no need to say you're sorry. I'm not telling you this to make you feel anything. I'm perfectly aware how you feel about a disabled child."

Kate was yelling, and I could *feel* her anger. Hurt and scorn spewed from her. I was determined that I was going to sit there, listen, and take it, no matter how much it hurt to hear her words. I was going to be a man, not a coward any longer.

"Delilah is my blessing. We are very happy, Adam. She's a wonderful baby. Yes, we have some big obstacles to overcome, but I wouldn't trade my life with her for a life with all of the so-called 'normal kids' in the world!"

I felt like I had slumped over in my chair and she was lashing me using an imaginary whip, one word after another.

"I'm sorry, Kate. I didn't mean to imply anything."

"You never do, Adam. I only asked you here to show you what you're missing, and nothing more."

"I know you have every right to be furious with me ..."

Kate interrupted me in the middle of my sentence and said without blinking an eye, "Are you ready to meet your daughter?" She picked up the baby monitor, and I could hear sounds coming from it. My heart started to beat faster.

I took a deep breath and said very timidly, "Yes, Kate,

I'm ready."

It was strange to be back in the home where we had shared twelve wonderful years. I saw that Kate had taken all of our pictures down. The color scheme was changed as well. It had gone from a cream-colored white to a pastel blue that was very calming. We passed the living room that now looked more like a child's playroom. Nothing looked like it did before.

I stopped suddenly to look at something familiar in the dining room. There on the wall was a picture of a bearded man sitting at a table praying. We had picked it up at a flea market when we first met. Kate had to have it. She said it would remind her to pray. I, on the other hand, never cared for it. Today, it brought a warm feeling over me. I almost felt as if I were home.

"I see you still have the praying man," I said with a slight smile.

Kate looked at me and said, "Yes, he wouldn't leave."

I followed Kate upstairs to the bedrooms. I couldn't help looking at the door that had led to our bedroom. It was closed. Across the hall, we entered a brightly-colored room decorated in rainbows. This used to be my study. Katie decorated it for me as a surprise on one of my birthdays. She said that if I were to become a big-time attorney, I would need my own space. She banned me from entering the room for a couple of months, and I had to refrain from peeking. When the big reveal came, Katie had placed a wide purple ribbon across the door. She said that I had to cut it. She giggled like a teenager as I walked into the room. It was truly wonderful. She had refinished an old oak desk. It had pens, tablets, a phone, and a picture of us on top of it. The curtains were mint green. A black love seat was against the wall. She even placed a small refrigerator in the room for cold drinks, so I would not have to make trips to the kitchen. At that moment, I knew how much she loved me. She said that every new room needed an initiation, and this one was no different. The love seat came in handy.

Looking around, I saw that it was now the baby's nursery. Once again, Kate had done a beautiful job. I looked over toward the crib, and there was Delilah. She was standing up and holding on to the side of the crib. Her hair was the exact red color that mine was as a child. It was curly and almost touched her shoulders.

I watched as Kate kissed Delilah's ear and picked her up in her arms. I moved closer, wanting to touch her. I stood behind Kate and saw that Delilah had beautiful green eyes. My heart was beating so fast that I thought it was going to come out of my chest. Here was this beautiful baby, and she was ours. For a moment, I forgot that she could neither see me nor hear me.

I followed Kate back to the living room and watched as she placed Delilah on the floor. Delilah took off crawling, making her way around the large area.

I asked Kate if she thought it would be okay if I got on

the floor with Delilah. Kate told me to approach her slowly and warned me that she might cry, since I was a stranger. For a split second, it felt like a knife going through my heart. The thought that I was indeed a stranger to my own child was hard to bear.

I got on the floor and approached Delilah just as Kate had instructed me. Delilah pulled herself up to a standing position and started banging her hands on the rocking horse. I reached out and touched her hair gently. She immediately stopped slapping the horse and turned her head from side to side.

"Hi, Delilah," I whispered.

"You know, Adam, that she can't hear you. But I do talk to her all the time as if she can," Kate explained. Kate got on the floor with me, took Delilah's hand, and placed it on my face, which has a short beard. Delilah jerked back her hand and let out a small grunt. Kate then took her hand once more and placed it on my face. Delilah grabbed the hair on my face, pulled hard, and then released my beard quickly.

I laughed loudly and saw out of the corner of my eye that Kate was actually smiling. Maybe she was hoping it had been painful.

"I guess I deserve that, and more," I said with a grin.

"Adam, there is so much to learn about Delilah, and I really don't want to waste your time."

I looked at Kate and then at Delilah and realized that my recurrent dream had been showing me my daughter and the world she lives in.

"Kate, I want to get to know Delilah. I promise that I will not leave again. I'm so sorry." Tears began to run down my cheeks. There was no stopping them this time. I sobbed like a baby. Then Katie did something I never expected. She reached over and touched my hand. I looked up to see tears in her eyes, too.

"Adam, if you're sure, then I'm willing to give you another chance."

Nothing in my life before then seemed to hold a candle to what was before me. I had no idea what the future would bring. I just knew that I wanted Delilah and Kate in my life. I didn't want Delilah to be in that field alone and without her daddy again.

Wiping the tears away, I said, "There's nothing that I want more."

Kate put her head down. I could tell that her hurt was still great. She had no reason to trust me at that point. Then she looked up and gave me a warning with instructions.

"Adam, please don't shave your beard. That will be how Delilah tells who you are. It will take some time and work on your part. If you're not in this for the long haul, I want you to know that you can leave right now." Kate looked at me with an intense look, unlike any I had seen before. I knew deep in my heart that this was the right thing. Delilah was my little girl, and I still loved her mother deeply.

I whispered, "I want to be here for you both."

    Kate reached down once more, placed Delilah's hand on my beard, and said the words I will never forget: "Delilah, meet your daddy."

Chapter Five

A Day at the Park

~ KATE ~

*S*ix months ago, Adam came back into our lives. He kept his word and has become a major part of Delilah's world. He moved back to town and makes a point of coming by after work every day to see her. Delilah knows her daddy. All she has to do is feel his beard for giggles and laughter to flow out of her body.

Adam is coming by today to take Delilah to the park. She loves going to the park and has always enjoyed that time with him. Adam asked me to think about joining them today, and I had to be honest: I would love nothing more. I heard a knock on the door and knew it must be him.

"Good morning, beautiful," said Adam.

I looked at him, grinned, and said, "I'm already going to the park, so no need to butter me up." Adam looked at me and put his hand on my face.

"It's all true. Are you and Delilah ready?"

I took Delilah out of her highchair where she had been eating her fill of Cheerios. She was wearing a pair of blue overalls with a large butterfly on the front. The shirt underneath was lime green, which made her red hair stand out. There was no combing her hair since it had a mind of its own. Adam came closer, took Delilah's tiny hand, and placed it on his beard. Delilah let out a squeal. She was smiling, and I could tell she was happy to know her daddy was here.

I watched as Adam picked her up, and she placed her little arms around his neck. I imagined how she must feel. I don't remember my father. I have had many dreams of having a daddy. I never wanted my daughter to grow up without a dad. I believe that every little girl needs her daddy.

And I have to be honest. I never wanted to turn away and let Adam walk out the door. My pride got in the way. I didn't even try to stop him. I didn't think about anything beyond my feelings having been hurt. Knowing Adam, he may have stopped, sat back down, and explained what he was feeling. I didn't give him any hope. I acted as if I neither needed him nor cared. I did need him, and I did love him.

After many days of rain, we were happy to step outside to find sunshine. The park was full of energetic children running around. The swings were taken for the moment, so we sat together on a bench, watching the other children play.

"Katie, do you ever wish Delilah could be one of those

children running around?"

I truly understood why he would ask that question. I also watched as the children ran around without a care in the world. I knew that Delilah's life would be different from their lives. I looked at Adam and could tell he was somewhat nervous about how I would respond. I wasn't often in the defensive mode anymore. Adam and I had come a long way. If we weren't able to be ourselves and speak about our fears, then we would end up right back where we had been before Adam left. I wanted Adam to talk to me and tell me what he was thinking.

"Yes. I do think about those things, too. I have the same concerns. I guess I look at our little world as a painting. You could take ten various artists and have each of them draw a picture of this park scene that we're enjoying. Each artist would have a different perspective of how it looks. One might see the homeless man over there, the dead tree branches, or the trash on the ground. Another artist might see the happy children's faces, the blue sky, and the family having a picnic on the grass. It's all in how we perceive the world. I want us to see nothing but the beautiful things in it and not to concentrate on the difficult things. Maybe we will be looking at our lives through rose-colored glasses, but honestly, what's wrong with that?"

Adam looked at me and smiled, "I knew there was a reason I fell in love with you."

"So, you are still in love with me?" I asked shyly.

Adam leaned over and kissed me sweetly on the lips. "I never stopped!"

It was then that Delilah, who was sitting in my lap, grabbed her daddy's beard as if to say, "Hey, I'm still here!"

Soon an empty swing came in sight, and we ran as quickly as we could to grab it.

"Hey, I have an idea. Let me sit in the swing and hold Delilah, and you can push us!" suggested Adam, laughing.

"Oh, I see how it is, equal opportunity on the swings," I retorted with a smile.

Adam got on the swing, and I placed Delilah snugly in his arms. I pushed the swing and listened to their laughter. I will never forget these moments. Suddenly, a thought hit me, sort of an epiphany. I wondered what Adam would say if I asked him to move in with Delilah and me. It would be nice to have him around all the time. I began to daydream about having our little family intact.

"Katie, are you quitting on me?"

"Huh? Oh, sorry. I was thinking about something."

"I can tell. You quit pushing the swing. Are you okay?"

"Adam, what would you think if I asked you to move in with Delilah and me?"

Adam put his feet out and stopped the swing abruptly. He looked at me with a startled look. I didn't give him a chance to answer and immediately started retracting my proposition. "Never mind. What I was thinking …"

"Katie …"

"I mean you have your own responsibilities and your work," I began to explain.

"Katie," Adam said again.

I looked up, and Adam was smiling. "I have to swing by the apartment and pack a bag or two. Is tonight too soon?"

I looked at Adam, and suddenly, I was bursting with excitement. "Does this mean …?"

"Katie, I want to be with you and Delilah forever," explained Adam gently.

We couldn't wait to leave the park. We swung by Adam's apartment, and Delilah and I waited in the car. I think Adam won the contest for the fastest person in the world to pack. He was packed and back in the car in less than twenty minutes.

"So, are you ready to do this?" I asked Adam.

"I am so ready to do this," Adam said.

In my mind, it made sense for Delilah to spend as much time with her daddy as she could. Since she had so many more obstacles ahead of her, we thought the consistency would be good for her. It would also help me, so that I wouldn't suffer burnout.

Adam moved into the spare room. My brother wasn't happy about the idea at first, but he and Adam have since managed to work out their relationship as well. Ben told Adam that if he ever hurt us again, he wouldn't be so nice the next time. I was sure he meant it, too.

Ben and Mia had gone back to Japan some time after

Delilah's birthday. A few months later, we received the call from them that they had two beautiful, healthy baby boys, Joshua and Jacob. This was the surprise Ben had wanted to share with me at Delilah's birthday party. He and Mia were expecting their first child, which turned out to be twins. Mia is lovely, and she and Ben are very happy living in Japan.

Adam asked me a curious question the other night. He asked if I ever resented the fact that Ben and Mia had two healthy babies. We almost got into a big argument because I jumped the gun thinking that Adam was comparing our Delilah to the boys. Thankfully, that wasn't the case. In fact, we had a sincere talk and realized that this was exactly the journey we had been given. We could either treat this time as a gift or carry around a woe-is-me mentality. We both agreed that our Delilah was a gift.

Teaching Delilah to walk was challenging, but it beat watching television. We spent our evenings having her sit between us on the floor. Each of us had shortbread cookies, the ones with a hole in the middle, on our fingers. We would stand Delilah up, and she would feel our hands. Recognizing one of her favorite treats, she would feel for the cookie and scream with delight when she got one off our finger. Then we would stand her up again and turn her around. She would reach straight ahead, feeling for the cookies. Each of us would gradually inch our way back.

One night Delilah took two steps and then three. She only had one speed: fast forward. She had fallen more times than I could count, had hit her head, and had cut her lip. And each time she got up and began again. She was amazing. She would make her way around the room, and as always, we would make sure that she could find us at the end of her walk. She cried only one time when the phone had rung, and I had gotten up to answer it. She completed her round, stopped, and realized I wasn't there in my normal spot. She let out a bloodcurdling scream. I couldn't imagine what she must have thought.

Delilah has learned some basic signs already such as cup, bath, eat, and goodbye. She and I always saw Adam off to work in the morning. Their routine for that morning goodbye was one that would touch the hardest of hearts. Adam knew I kept late nights working for the paper, so he suggested that I sleep in and let him take care of the early-morning routines. He didn't have to be at the office until nine. It took me a long time to get used to this. I found myself lying wide awake, listening for any signs of trouble. It wasn't easy to give up control and trust someone else to take care of Delilah.

Every weekday, Adam turned off his alarm, took a shower, and started the coffee. He then made his way into Delilah's room where she would be standing in the crib waiting. He would lean close to her, and she would grab his beard. He would shake his head back and forth, and Delilah thought this was a great game. Then he had to pry her hands from his beard.

The challenge was on when he tapped her bottom for a

diaper change. She was too big for the changing table, so she was placed on a mat on the floor. Delilah wouldn't lie there but wanted to get up and run. We were unsure where she thought she was going. We have had to take measures to keep her safe and to remember always to close the door.

Mrs. Hamilton has continued to come to work with Delilah and has become a part of our family. I don't know where we would be without her. Adam and Mrs. Hamilton have bumped heads a couple of times, just as Mrs. Hamilton and I have. She has had to let him learn by letting go. She didn't mind Adam living with us but kept asking when we were going to get married. We looked at her, shrugged our shoulders, and changed the subject. That was the last thing on our minds right then.

Sometimes I would lie in bed at night and think about how much I wanted to hear Delilah say, "Momma." Mrs. Hamilton had become my best friend and could be such a good listener when I was feeling down. I confided my thoughts to her more than I should have, I know. Mrs. Hamilton always said that I needed to put that out of my mind. She reminded me that Delilah would learn the word "Momma," and it would be music to my hands. She said that an orchestra's conductor never says a word, that his hands direct the beautiful music. And so it would be for Delilah. She would be a conductor. As her hands directed the symphony of life, beautiful things would happen. I just had to believe.

Chapter Six

The Ferry Ride

~ ADAM ~

*B*eing a new dad had been a life-changing event for me. Life was no longer about me but about my family and putting them first.

One of my first transitions was exchanging my sleek Mercedes convertible for a Tahoe. It only took one trip to town to show me that we needed something bigger. Kate's old car was on its last leg and was not reliable to get her and Delilah around.

Moving in with Kate and Delilah was my second life-changing transition. We had lived together for 12 years, but we were different people now. We had a baby. When Kate had asked me to move in that day in the park, my mouth fell open in surprise. I thought at first that she was coming around, remembering the way we had been. But it wasn't about us. She made that clear. It was for Delilah. She admitted to feeling worn down, and I had noticed that she was looking more tired lately.

Being an attorney afforded me many possessions and a certain lifestyle, but all of the material things in this world could not have filled the emptiness I felt inside. I had never thought I was the best-looking person, but Kate must have seen something in me at one time. I had a balding head now and only by the grace of God could I still grow a beard. It had silver all through it. I had red hair in my younger days, but those days were gone. I wore glasses and couldn't see anything without them. Being six feet tall let me carry that extra twenty or thirty pounds around my middle.

I was more of a reader, the quiet, observant type. I had been thinking about reading to Delilah. Sadness loomed over me as I realized the futility of the one passion I wouldn't be able to share with her. Mrs. Hamilton said that one day Delilah would learn Braille. For that, I was thankful, but it could never replace my little girl sitting on my lap hearing me read to her. Seeing her point to the farm animals on the page and making their sounds was all part of sharing these special moments in time.

I guess I did have some worries, but I kept them to myself. I would never share them with Kate. Mrs. Hamilton asked me what I was waiting for. I didn't understand what she meant. She asked why I had not read to Delilah. I told her that Delilah couldn't hear me, and I would be reading for myself. That was when she threw her hands in the air and stormed out of the kitchen. I really didn't understand why she got so angry with me. She mumbled something like, "He still does not get it!" What was I not getting?

Kate had to catch up on a lot of work from the paper, so I offered to take care of Delilah all day. It took some persuading, but she finally gave in. I told her to lock herself in her room and let me handle things. If I needed her, I would yell, ring a bell, or something.

It was a beautiful Saturday morning, and my first thought was that we had to get out of the house. I presented the idea to Kate, and she actually agreed and wished us a good time. She kissed Delilah, gave me a nice pat on my shoulder, and retreated upstairs to her room. Delilah was finishing her breakfast, so I began to pack her a little bag. I placed the small chain in Delilah's hand, and her little feet started swinging as she sported the grin that I loved so much. She knew it was time to go outside to the park.

It was early spring, and the sun was shining brightly. Since we lived outside of San Francisco, the weather still demanded a sweater at that time of year. Thankfully, the fog had lifted, and clear skies loomed overhead. I placed Delilah in her car seat and put her vibrating caterpillar in her hands. She was as happy as could be. Then I put her little pink sunglasses on her face. She has gotten used to wearing them. Just as I finished getting her settled, I noticed her signing for her cup. I had to take a second look. I couldn't believe it! She was telling me she wanted a drink. I started yelling for Kate.

"Kate! Kate!" I cried. She poked her head out the upstairs window.

"Are you okay? What's wrong?" Kate yelled back down.

"Delilah just signed 'cup' and wants me to give her a drink," I called happily.

"That's wonderful," yelled Kate. "So give her a drink." Kate laughed and waved goodbye.

I reached into the diaper bag, pulled out the sippy cup, and placed it in Delilah's hands. I couldn't tell you what that moment did for me. It confirmed that inside our little girl was a person who just needed the tools to learn to communicate. Delilah told me what she needed, and I was able to give it to her. The feeling was something that I can't put into words.

Soon, we were on our way. I happened to look over to my right and saw the Bay Bridge. Noticing the Golden Gate Ferries, an idea came to my mind. How wonderful it would be to take Delilah on a ferry ride and let her feel the wind and mist on her face! I made the decision: we would take the ferry from the Golden Gate Bridge, traveling around Angel Island, Marin's hill towns, and lastly, Mount Tamaulipas. Part of me was a bit nervous. Should I call Kate and tell her about our upcoming adventure, or take the chance of facing her wrath later? I threw caution to the winds, and Delilah and I boarded the ferry. I carried her to the back of the ferry and stood on the balcony waiting for the departure.

A well-meaning, little elderly woman attempted to talk to Delilah, but Delilah paid no attention to her and only held on to me tightly. Delilah appeared content because she knew I was holding her, but she was aware that we were somewhere unfamiliar. "Cute baby," the elderly woman said, looking at Delilah.

"Thank you," I replied.

Delilah looked out past the woman as if she wasn't there. By the expression on the elderly woman's face, I could tell that she was aware something was not right. I decided to put her mind at ease since I realized that she was too kind to ask.

"Delilah is blind and deaf, so I thought I would let her experience a nice ride on the ferry today," I explained.

I wasn't sure if I needed to explain, or if this was the right thing to do, but deep down I knew I had nothing to be ashamed of. I understood the importance of people being introduced to Delilah, and through the process, they would understand and get to know her. Yes, I wanted the world to meet Delilah.

"I thought your little one was not looking at me, but I thought maybe it was this old face scaring her," she said with a laugh. "The look on her face looked so familiar to me. You know, I had a brother who was blind," the elderly woman explained. "Back then, it wasn't talked about. He didn't have proper training, and my mum and dad kept him inside. They loved him and protected him too much. He learned to read and loved books, but they never let him go outside our home. I was a couple of years older, and I would spend many hours playing with him. He was a smart boy, he was. I asked my mum one day if I could take him outside. She let me take him to the grass. He was about eight years old. I remember him lying on the grass, and he started to cry. I asked him, 'Why you crying, Joey Boy?' That was what I called him back then. He told me, 'I read in one of my books about grass, but I never knew we had any.' "

Tears began to fill her eyes as she continued to tell her story. "One day Joey Boy decided to go outside to lie in the grass but wandered too far and fell into the lake. He didn't know how to swim. Me mum always blamed herself. Our lives were never the same after that. I think if he had been taught about the world and what was outside, then he would have known not to go to the lake. The grass would have been just grass because it would have been normal for him. So, young man, you take care of that baby. Teach and show her everything. Today is a good start."

The elderly woman took Delilah's hands and kissed them. Then she turned and walked to the other side of the boat. I could tell she was crying.

The ferry began to move. A spray of water hit our faces, and the wind felt cool. Delilah trusted her daddy. She was quiet, squinted her eyes, and wrinkled up her nose as the mist of water sprayed on her face. She was holding her caterpillar tightly. I had her diaper bag on one arm and Delilah in the other. I pulled her hood over her head and held her tightly. Delilah wrapped her little arm around my neck but didn't make a sound.

Out of the blue, I heard Mrs. Hamilton's voice as she stomped out of the kitchen: "He just does not get it," she had said. I smiled to myself and thought, *Mrs. Hamilton, I finally get it. I really do.* I thought about the sweet elderly woman and the words she had spoken to me: "Teach and show her everything." That is my job as her father, not only to protect her, but also to show her the world.

Suddenly, my phone rang. It was Kate. "Adam, are you and Delilah coming home soon? I've made some chili."

I had thought I could get away with taking this little adventure without getting the third degree. "We should be home soon, maybe in another hour," I explained. I knew better than to think the conversation would end there, and I was fully prepared for her to yell at me.

"Adam, where are you?" asked Kate sharply.

"Uh, well, we kind of took a ferry ride," I said with caution. There was dead silence on the other end of the phone. "Kate, are you there?"

I then heard a very timid, "Yes," on the line.

"Are you okay?" I asked.

Surprisingly, Kate said, "I hope you and Delilah have a great time. See you soon." I was shocked at her response. I couldn't help but smile. Kate trusted me, and that meant everything to me.

The ferry ride took us around the bay, and the sun settled on the horizon. It was time to go home. Delilah had fallen asleep in my arms. I made my way back to the Tahoe and gently placed her in the car seat. I kissed her forehead, slipped the caterpillar from her arms, and laid it beside her on the seat. I gave Kate a quick call and told her we were on our way home.

"Katie, I just want to say thanks."

"For what?" Kate asked.

"Thank you for giving me such a beautiful daughter. Thank you for trusting me again, and thank you for being an awesome mom."

Kate was silent for a moment and then said laughing, "I don't know what you ate on the ferry, but I'll make sure you have it again."

When Delilah and I arrived at home. Katie took the sleepy girl and laid her down in her bed. The table was set, and the chili smelled wonderful. We sat down across from each other at the table.

"How was the ferry ride?" Kate asked.

I looked at her intently and began to tell her about the elderly woman on the ferry. I continued to explain to Kate what she had told me about her brother and the words of wisdom she had shared with me.

"I think Mrs. Hamilton will be very proud of you, Adam," Kate said, reaching across the table to touch my hand. "I'm very proud of you, too."

I leaned over the table and looked into Kate's eyes. "I really meant everything I said on the phone. You have no idea what this means to me. We are going to be a great family, and I promise I will never, ever let you down again."

Katie leaned closer, and our lips met. It was the sweetest kiss. It was familiar, and one that I had longed for. I knew in my heart that we were on our way to rebuilding what we had lost.

Chapter Seven

Goodbye, Love

~ ADAM ~

*K*atie and I woke up early. We both had very busy days planned. Kate had an appointment at Liberty School for the Blind in hopes of getting Delilah enrolled. I had a long list of clients to see. After quick kisses goodbye, I drove in one direction, and Kate and Delilah drove in the other.

One of my meetings, a divorce case, proved to be a nightmare. Between their outbursts of anger, I was aware of an uneasy feeling in my gut. My mind was on Kate and Delilah. I tried to push the feeling away and realized that I just wanted this day to end so I could go home.

The last year and a half with Kate and Delilah had flown by. Delilah was almost three. My clientele had picked up, but the extra work caused me to work later, and I'm not happy about that.

I looked at my watch and realized I hadn't heard from Kate. She and Delilah should have been heading back home by now from the appointment with the school. If everything had gone as planned, Delilah should be able to start in their pre-kindergarten program, since she would be turning three soon. Their appointment was at one o'clock. Kate should have called by now. I looked out the window. The thunderstorm had not let up. Suddenly, my cell phone rang. I excused myself from the meeting and answered the call.

"Hello, is this Mr. Bennett?"

"Yes," I replied.

"Mr. Bennett, you need to come to Memorial Hospital. Your daughter and her mother have been in an accident."

I felt instant panic and broke out in a sweat. "What happened? Are they okay?"

"Please come, Mr. Bennett. We will explain everything when you get here."

Hanging up the phone, my heart felt like it would pound out of my chest. I looked at the couple and at the other attorney and apologized. I explained that I had an emergency. I didn't even give them time to respond. I slammed the door behind me.

Oh, my God. Something terrible has happened. I can feel it!

I rushed to the hospital as fast as I could. Leaving the car running, I ran into the emergency room entrance and approached the front desk. "Please, my name is Adam

Bennett. Kate Moore has just been admitted with my daughter, Delilah Moore!"

"Please calm down, Mr. Bennett, and let me check our records. While I'm looking, please go park your car. I promise I will have the information for you as soon as you return."

I looked back and realized that I had left the car running and the car door wide open. The rain continued to come down hard. The feeling in my gut told me something was terribly wrong. I turned around reluctantly and headed out the door to park the car. When I came back into the emergency room, I was soaked to the skin. The woman behind the desk was standing with another woman who reached out her hand to shake mine.

"Mr. Bennett, my name is Helen Flores. Please follow me to my office."

"What's going on?" I asked nervously, as I followed her down the long hall.

"I will explain, Mr. Bennett. Please come in." She pointed to the open office door. "Please sit down, Mr. Bennett."

I slowly sat down in the chair across from her desk and could feel my body shaking.

"Mr. Bennett, I'm afraid I have some very bad news," said Mrs. Flores.

I could feel a lump beginning to form in my throat.

"This is not easy to say, Mr. Bennett. Kate Moore and Delilah, whom I understand to be your daughter, have been in a terrible car wreck."

I stood up and felt like the room was spinning out of control. I didn't want to ask the next question. "Are they okay? Where are they? I want to see them!"

"I'm so sorry, Mr. Bennett, but I'm afraid that Kate didn't make it," explained Mrs. Flores sadly. "We have contacted Kate's next of kin, whom I believe is her brother Ben. I spoke with him, and he will be on the next plane back to the States. He's the one who gave me your number and explained that Delilah is your daughter."

"Oh, God, no! Please tell me this is not true," I cried out with uncontrolled emotions. I doubled over, feeling as if I had been hit in the stomach. I felt as if I were going to be sick. The pain was almost too much for me to bear. "Not my Katie!"

Mrs. Flores stood by my side and placed her hand on my shoulder. I flung her hand off and asked sternly, "Where is my daughter?" I was numb. This couldn't be true. Why was this woman torturing me? This must have been a bad dream, and I was not able to wake up.

"She is in our children's ward. She has some scrapes and bruises, but other than that, she seems okay. We haven't been able to calm her down. She has been crying for the last four hours until she finally fell asleep."

I looked up at Mrs. Flores who was now wiping tears from her eyes.

"I want to see her, now!" I demanded with tears streaming down my cheeks. I felt like I was going to lose it at any moment.

"Of course," Mrs. Flores said gently. And once again, she said, "I am so very sorry."

My legs and arms felt heavy. I followed Mrs. Flores down the hall in a daze. I stopped suddenly and stated, "I want to see Kate first. Where is she?"

Mrs. Flores turned toward me and said, "Certainly. I will take you to Kate."

On the way to the morgue, Mrs. Flores told me that they had moved her from the emergency room to the morgue downstairs. She explained that Kate was already gone when they brought her to the ER. The next of kin was Ben, but since he was out of the country, everything was on hold. I had no legal authority, and she could only let me say goodbye. Ben had to sign all of the necessary paperwork.

We took the elevator to the bottom floor and began the long walk to the end of the sterile, cold hallway. She knocked on the door and spoke with the man in a green lab coat. His solemn expression was not a surprise. Escorted to the back room, I saw a body draped with a white sheet. I stopped. I wasn't sure I could do this.

As I drew closer, the man with the green lab coat asked me if I were ready. I nodded my head. He gently pulled the sheet away from Kate's head. There she was, my lovely, beautiful Katie. She looked like she was sleeping. I reached out and touched her face. I kissed her forehead, and then I couldn't stop the tears from flowing. The wailing that came from my soul seemed as if it were coming from someone else. The hurt I felt at that moment was indescribable.

I leaned closer to Kate and whispered, "Do not worry, my love. I will take care of our Delilah. I promise I will make you proud."

I looked up and nodded to the man in the green lab coat. He covered Kate's face, and I turned and walked away. Mrs. Flores was waiting for me. She put her arm around my shoulder, and we walked down the long corridor to the waiting elevator.

Mrs. Flores looked at me, smiled, and said, "Let's go see your daughter. She needs you."

I remembered that a paternity test had never been done on Delilah and that I was not recorded on her birth certificate. I wasn't sure if there was anything I could do legally at this moment for my baby girl.

I am an attorney, for God's sake, and I don't even have my affairs in order. Adam, you stupid fool!

We got on the elevator, and Mrs. Flores pushed the button for the seventh floor. The doors opened to a brightly decorated children's floor. The nurses looked up from their desk, and Mrs. Flores explained that I was Delilah's father. She escorted me to the last room on the right. I looked in and saw Delilah in the crib on her knees. She was rocking back and forth and crying in a low moan. I walked closer and reached down to pick her up. She immediately started screaming in terror. I grabbed her hands quickly and placed them on my beard. She tried to stop crying when she realized it was her daddy. She wrapped her little arms around my neck, holding on tightly. She cried quietly for the next hour. I held her tightly as I sat in the rocker. And I continued to hold her through the night.

I must have fallen asleep with Delilah still in my arms. She was fast asleep when I awoke. I got up and gently laid her back in the crib. I looked at the clock on the wall, and it was midnight. Then I realized that I had not called Mrs. Hamilton. She was so close to Kate. I had to call her. I dialed her number, and when she answered, I could tell she had been asleep.

"Mrs. H, it's me, Adam. Please come to Memorial Hospital. I cannot talk to you on the phone."

Without a word, I heard a dial tone. I knew she was on her way.

A nurse peeked in, asked if I was okay, and looked at Delilah. As she turned to leave the room, I said, "Nurse, I have a request. I need to get a paternity test done in the morning. Can you please write a note to the doctor? I have to make sure that I can take my daughter home once she's discharged."

She looked at me and said she would pass the message on to the doctor on call.

Just about that time, the phone rang. It was Ben. He would be landing at around six o'clock that evening. I told him I would pick him up. No other words were spoken, and we both hung up quickly. I stood over Delilah's crib and watched her as she slept. Such a sweet baby, I thought to myself. She was almost three and growing fast. I just didn't know what kind of God would take her mother away. I had always been a believer, but now I was questioning everything. It was too cruel, too mean, and not the God I thought I knew.

I was startled when I felt a hand on my shoulder. Mrs. Hamilton was standing behind me. My eyes began to fill with tears. I grabbed her, sobbing uncontrollably, and told her that Kate was gone. She began to cry, and I didn't know what to say or do. We sat in the dark, holding hands, for over two hours without saying anything. Then I looked at Mrs. Hamilton, with tears coming down my face, and I felt angry.

"I don't know how a loving God could take a mother from her deaf and blind child. I'm so angry, Mrs. H," I said as I cried some more.

Mrs. Hamilton got up, took my face in her hands, and began to say these words. "Adam, I promise I am hurting, too. I don't say too much about my beliefs, but I can tell you with certainty that God is a loving Father just like you, and I am sure He is sharing in our sorrow. It doesn't matter that Delilah is blind and deaf. We all are blind and deaf until we feel the touch of God's love. Circumstances, good and bad, make us who we are. Kate touched all of us. Her faith was strong, and she would want you to know that God loves you, even in this horrible situation."

"I'm sorry, Mrs. H. I just don't see it that way." I looked away and wiped my tears on my sleeve. Mrs. Hamilton began to cry. I was amazed that, even through her tears, she was still holding on to her faith in God.

I turned toward her and said, "I'm sorry. I know you're hurting, too."

"In time, Adam, you will understand. In time. For now, just rest," Mrs. Hamilton explained as she wiped the tears from her eyes.

Mrs. Hamilton pulled a chair beside Delilah's crib. We sat in silence once more.

At about five o'clock, before daylight, a nurse came into the room. "Mr. Bennett, we're here to take your blood sample. We will need to wake Delilah as well." After they took the sample from me, I picked up Delilah. She barely stirred as they swabbed her mouth. She was exhausted.

Mrs. Hamilton was curious as to what this was for, and I explained about the paternity test. The nurse told us that the results should be in soon. Once they had determined I was the father, they would release Delilah to go home. Mrs. Hamilton offered to come home with us. I gladly took her up on her offer, knowing there was so much I didn't know. I explained that Ben was flying in that night.

"Adam," Mrs. Hamilton asked, "I'm sorry to ask, but where is Kate now?"

I looked at Mrs. Hamilton and could barely get the words out. "They have moved her to the funeral home. Ben made the arrangements. I believe there will be a memorial service tomorrow."

Mrs. Hamilton decided she would go to the funeral home at ten o'clock the next morning. Slowly making her way inside, Mrs. Hamilton sat in the chapel waiting for Jim, the mortician, to come speak with her. Mrs. Hamilton had known Jim for many years, and Jim had completed Kate's wishes to be cremated.

"Judy, I'm sorry, but Kate was cremated early this morning. If I had known, I could have held off just a while longer."

"I know, Jim. Do you mind if I just sit here for a while?"

"By all means," Jim said gently. "I have a necklace that Kate was wearing if you would like to have it."

"Is it the cross with a diamond in the center?" Mrs. Hamilton asked.

"Yes, it is, a very lovely cross," said Jim.

"I gave that to Kate on her birthday this past year. I'll save it for Delilah."

Jim placed the cross in Mrs. Hamilton's hands and gently closed her hands over it.

"Jim, Kate was the daughter I never had. I loved her so," explained Mrs. Hamilton. She opened her hand to look at the cross.

"I'm so sorry, Judy. God bless you," Jim said sadly, as he walked away.

Mrs. Hamilton walked up to the front of the chapel and looked up at the lighted picture of Christ hanging on the cross. "I'm going to need your help on this one, Lord."

Mrs. Hamilton returned to the hospital where I was sitting with Delilah. I shared with her that the tests confirmed I was indeed Delilah's father and that discharge papers were on their way.

"I had no doubt," said Mrs. Hamilton smiling.

We were surprised when a police officer showed up in Delilah's room. He said there were some items in the car that he thought we would want. In the bag were Delilah's caterpillar, a sippy cup, Kate's purse, and a blue folder. He offered his condolences. I asked if he knew exactly what had happened, but he said he couldn't be sure of all the details. He did know that an elderly man was driving the other car and had cut in front of them. He had suffered a heart attack and, in fact, had died this morning. Knowing the details didn't make me feel any better. All I could do then was picture the horrific scene, knowing that I was not there to hold Kate in her final moments.

The nurse came in, and I was able to sign all of the paperwork for discharge. By then, Delilah had awakened and was very fussy. Nothing I could do was helping. I realized that she was missing Kate. Mrs. Hamilton brought out her red heart and placed the heart in Delilah's hands. Delilah reached her arms out to Mrs. Hamilton. She took Delilah and held her close. I packed all that we had, and we left the hospital for home.

It was about two o'clock in the afternoon when we arrived home. We opened the door, and both of us stood outside the door, not knowing what to do next. Mrs. Hamilton touched my face and said, "Adam, one step at a time, love. One step at a time."

I put one foot forward, and we walked into the house, knowing our lives would never be the same.

It wasn't long before I had to make my way to pick up Ben up at the airport. I was not ready to face Kate's brother. I knew he would be grief stricken. He didn't want to see Kate's body. He wanted to remember her the way she was.

Ben was standing outside the terminal when I pulled up. He got into the car and said very little. The drive was heart wrenching. Neither one of us knew what to say. Finally, Ben broke the silence.

"Adam, I am so sorry for both of us, but most of all I am sorry for Delilah. Kate loved her so much," Ben explained through his tears.

"I know, Ben. I promise that she will never forget the love of her mother. I will find a way always to tell her about her mom. I just have to figure out how," I explained sadly.

No other words were exchanged. There was nothing more to say. Once we arrived at the house, Ben went straight to Delilah. Without a thought, he picked Delilah up from her crib while she slept and sat in the rocker by the window, rocking her for the next couple of hours. Kate's picture lay on the table beside the rocker. It was one of her and Delilah when she was born. Tears flowed freely down Ben's cheeks. All he could think about was that his little sister was gone.

The memorial service for Kate was brief. A few close friends came to say goodbye. Kate and I had discussed many years ago that we wanted our ashes thrown into the Bay. After the service, we all boarded the boat I had chartered from which we would spread Kate's ashes. Ben held Delilah, and Mrs. Hamilton held tightly to my arm. Beth and Eddie stood looking out at the water.

Eddie asked if he could say a few words. "I have never been one for words. I know it's funny to hear that since I own a paper and all, but I mean words from the heart. I want you all to know that Kate was like the daughter I never had. I loved her so much, and I am going to miss her." Eddie stepped back and couldn't go on. Beth put her arms around him.

Ben cleared his throat and attempted to speak, but no words came. He said, "I'm sorry ... she knows." And he pulled Delilah close.

Mrs. Hamilton looked at everyone and attempted to offer some words of comfort. "Kate was a special lady. I loved her so. She was a great mother and friend. I'm sure she will be near us in her own way, looking down on us all."

Mrs. Hamilton looked at me, and I knew I had to say something. "I am angry, I won't lie. I am damned angry, but

Kate wouldn't want me to be like this. She would want me to be a good father, not a bitter father, so I'm putting my anger aside. I am going to honor her life by being the best dad I can be to Delilah. I love you, Kate."

Each person threw some of Kate's ashes into the water. Then each of us gently released yellow flowers into the water. We watched as they floated away until we could see them no more.

Ben, Mrs. Hamilton, and I had a small gathering at the house. Ben and I were able to talk for a couple of hours about Kate and about Delilah's future. He reassured me that he and his family would always be a part of our lives. I felt good about that because all of my family is gone now, except for Delilah and Mrs. Hamilton. I found comfort in his words. Ben flew back to Japan the next day.

A week had passed since Kate's death, and life without her had been a big adjustment. It was not as if I could just sit down and quit. As much as I wanted to give up and hide myself away, I couldn't for the sake of Delilah. She became my lifeline, my reason to get up in the morning. Mrs. Hamilton stayed with us and took over the morning duties. I moved my office to the house, and it has worked out fine. I really haven't started back to work just yet, but I thought it would be best to work from home for a while.

The blue folder that Kate left behind contained all of Delilah's registration paperwork from the school, and Delilah was due to start in two weeks. She would be in school all day. At the Liberty School for the Blind, they would teach her Braille and other modes of communication. Mrs. Hamilton was going to start teaching me to sign as well. I knew some basic signs, but I had to be able to keep up.

I've noticed some strange things happening in the house lately, and I'm not sure what to think of them. I walked into Delilah's room one day after she took her nap, and she was laughing and reaching out to the air. I watched because she seemed to be communicating with someone. Some people might think I'm being overly sensitive, but I thought for a moment that maybe Kate was watching over Delilah. We don't understand much about the darkness in which Delilah lives. She is very sensitive to the world around her. I wouldn't be surprised if the two had connected somehow. Perhaps Kate is now Delilah's guardian angel. Oh, how I wish that could be true.

Another strange instance was with Mrs. Hamilton. She told me that she went in to get Delilah up in the morning, and her vibrating caterpillar was on. She remembered distinctly turning it off the night before to save the batteries. Mrs. Hamilton swears that Kate is looking over Delilah.

On the first Saturday without Kate, I asked Mrs. Hamilton if she would like to go into San Francisco with us and walk the Wharf. It was a beautiful day, and it would be nice just to get out. She told me she really needed to run some errands and that I didn't need an old woman tagging along.

"Good morning, beautiful girl," I told Delilah as she gave a quick tug on my beard. She was smiling and seemed to be in a happy mood. I changed her diaper, got her dressed, and headed to the kitchen. I turned quickly when I thought I heard Kate's voice. I swear I heard her whisper, "Adam." Maybe I was hearing things.

The first morning without Mrs. Hamilton was very quiet throughout the house. As I placed Delilah in her highchair, I happened to see an envelope lying on the counter. It had my name on it. I opened it up and had to sit down quickly because my heart was beating so fast. It was a letter from Kate. I looked around, knowing I didn't put it there. Maybe it was Mrs. Hamilton, or Ben. Yes, that has to be it. I slowly opened the letter and read Kate's words.

Dear Adam,

I have wanted to give you this letter for some time now, but I got scared and tucked it away. I have been waiting for the perfect time. I just want you to know how proud I am of the way you have taken on Delilah and me. You are such a fantastic dad. I forgive you for the past. It is over and done. I want you to let it go. What counts is the here and now. I do see myself married to you one day, and I would be proud to be your wife. You and Delilah are all I have ever wanted. Life is short, and we should never forget to tell someone how much we love them. I am telling you today in this letter that, Adam Bennett, I truly love you.

Love, Kate

Tears flowed down my face. I whispered, "I love you, too, Kate." I wanted to tell her so many times. Why did I not tell her? I slowly put the letter back into the envelope and looked over at Delilah. She was sitting very still. I watched her as she watched something in her dark world. I would like to think that she could see colors, ponies, dancing clowns, and other beautiful things that might live in her world. I didn't like to think that she was alone in total darkness and silence. In her world, she could hear and see. In her world, Kate was still with her. I looked at her and realized how much she looked like her mommy, except for my red hair.

"I love you, Delilah," I said. I placed my hand inside her palm and signed, "I love you."

She stopped, grabbed my hand, and signed, "Cup." I laughed loudly and thought that was a good start. Smiling at my little girl, I said to her, "A cup full of love coming right up."

Chapter Eight

Liberty School for the Blind

~ MRS. HAMILTON ~

*T*ime has gone by so fast. It seems like it was only yesterday when Kate first called me to work with Delilah. I never dreamed that I would end up helping Adam and that Kate would no longer be on this earth. Even though she is gone, she will forever be in our hearts.

The last three years of working with Delilah and her little family have been such a pleasure. Kate and Adam have been like family to me. When Kate died, I thought, "My poor little Delilah. How can Adam possibly manage without Kate?" I have since realized that the love Adam has for his little girl can move mountains. He is a gem.

Today, I wanted to introduce Adam to my side of the world, beyond the walls of his home. I have two grown sons, Michael and Brandon, and I wanted Adam to meet them.

Michael was my firstborn and is now 40 years old. I was twenty years old when he was born. During my pregnancy, I suffered from a horrible case of rubella that caused blindness and deafness in Michael.

My husband worked long hours for the railroad, leaving me alone with Michael. His job did afford me the luxury of staying at home to work with Michael. I read every book I could get my hands on, and Helen Keller's was one that inspired me most. I realized very early on that anything was possible. I learned to sign on my own and taught Michael before he ever went to school. I gave him a small cane to find his way at two and a half. I can't tell you how many things got broken or the bruises that were left on my legs. It just so happened that we were near one of the oldest deaf-and-blind schools in the country in the great state of Virginia. We lived only twenty miles from the school. You might call it divine intervention, but whatever it was, I was extremely thankful.

When Michael turned three, I drove him to the school's day program Monday through Friday. I also worked there as a volunteer. That's where I learned many of my skills. I still remember the first day we walked into the school. They were awed that a three-year-old child could find his way around with a cane. He could already sign the very basic signs. I felt very proud of both of us. We never wanted Michael to live there, but that was an option once he turned five.

When Michael was eight years of age, I got my first job

working for the school. It was then that I found myself working with a little boy named Brandon who was five at the time. He was a ward of the state and lived at the school. Brandon stole my heart right away. Michael was the one who told me I should bring Brandon home. Michael signed that he wanted a brother. My husband and I talked about it, and we agreed that this was the thing to do.

My Oliver had always been a gentle man and one who loved his boys. He did his best when he was home. Oliver died of a heart attack when Michael was only ten years old. Brandon had just turned seven. Oliver left me a small widow's pension to take care of the two boys. How we ended up in San Francisco is a whole other story, but I will get back to that. Needless to say, I understand the anguish that Adam is going through, suddenly finding himself all alone.

I still stand amazed at what my boys have been able to accomplish, and I would like for Adam to see this. I spoke with him about it, and he was willing to take a trip into the city with me to visit Michael and Brandon. The boys share a small apartment on the east side. Mr. Jones, a volunteer for people with disabilities, picks up the boys every morning and drives them to the school. He has done this for the last ten years. At the end of the day, he is there waiting for them. He assists with grocery shopping, doctor appointments, and many other things the boys need.

Mr. Jones' wife Mitzi actually worked with the boys when they moved out into the community. She spent many years helping them become independent. Mitzi was one of the most kindhearted women I have ever met. I continued to work with others while she worked with my boys. Michael and Brandon always wanted to be teachers, so they stayed on course through high school and college. After graduating from high school, they wanted to move into their own apartment. As most mothers would be, I was scared to death, but they wanted to be independent. Even though I knew they had a lot of common sense and were very smart, I worried about how they would be able to live on their own, work part-time at the blind school, and keep up with their college studies.

One day, the boys and I were having a celebration dinner in the city for their high school graduation, and I noticed that a woman was watching us as we signed, smiled, and laughed. Mitzi and Mr. Jones were at the table beside ours. Mitzi approached our table and said she didn't mean to interrupt. She explained that she was a community volunteer for people with disabilities. Then she asked if there was anything we needed.

Brandon knew someone had approached the table and signed, "Is there a problem?"

Mitzi immediately started signing back to him, and before I knew it, they were having a long conversation. Then Michael joined in. Finally, they stopped talking, and Mitzi said, "The boys want to move out on their own, and I would be glad to make that happen!"

I looked across the table and both boys were smiling broadly. I was shocked that this was what they had talked about for so long. We agreed to meet with Mitzi, and she shared with us about the process. One week later, we met in her home. She didn't have an office or a calling card. What she did have was a big heart that had helped many others throughout the years to live independently.

The plan went like this. Since the boys would be attending college and working at the school in the fall, she wanted an apartment nearby. An intervener would attend college with them. All summer, they would learn everything about their surroundings. In the fall, she would pick them up every morning and take them to the college campus where their intervener would be waiting. At one o'clock, she would pick them up and take them over to Liberty School where they would tutor the younger children. Mitzi would teach them how to cook and to depend on each other. She would take them anywhere they needed to go.

The apartment they secured had many things made especially for the boys. Mr. Jones did most of the work, such as the raised lettering on the cabinets, food containers, and other items. Everything had a place. Of course, I checked on them many times during the week but tried not to take over. I knew they had to find their way, but I was there if they needed me.

At seven o'clock in the morning, I arrived at the house

to find Delilah and Adam waiting. Adam had dressed Delilah in a cute pink top with jeans. Her little brown boots graced her feet. He had put her hair up in pigtails with pink bows. Adam had become the professional in dealing with Delilah's curly locks.

"Good morning, handsome, and my little love," I said as I received a quick peck on the cheek from Adam. He was such a sweetheart. I could see what Kate saw in him. I am an old woman, but if I were younger, I would certainly have eyes for him. I am content, however, to fill the gap of surrogate momma/grandma/teacher/friend to both Delilah and Adam.

I took out my red heart and placed it in Delilah's hands. She got excited and extended her arms out to me. I took her from Adam and gave her a big hug. We walked out to the car, and after Adam placed Delilah in her car seat, I handed her the caterpillar she loved. We settled ourselves in the car and were on our way.

"Mrs. H, please tell me about your sons. How did you get to San Francisco?" Adam asked.

"It's a rather long story, but I will try to condense it for your sake," I told him, chuckling. "After Oliver died, it was not easy. Even though I made a good living from my small widow's pension and working at the school, I really wanted a change. It was hard to live in the same house and the same town with all of my memories. One day on our bulletin board at the school, there was a newspaper clipping saying that Liberty School for the Blind had opened up in San Francisco. I wrote them a long letter describing my years of teaching, and I guess they liked what they read. It wasn't easy back then to find people who were educated in this field. I explained about my boys, who were then twelve and fifteen, and about my being a widow. I also told them about my years of working experience. I received a letter from the school stating that they wanted to hire me. I packed up my boys, moved to San Francisco, rented a small apartment a couple of blocks from the school, and went to work. The best part was that the boys could attend the school free.

"After the boys graduated from high school, they attended the local college and received their teaching certificates. Both boys live independently and work full-time as teachers at Liberty School. They have worked hard to get where they are. It wasn't easy, but education and communication skills are the key. From the beginning, I told them that they could do whatever they set their minds to do. Being an intervener for the school led me to work with Delilah in your home. I guess you could say I was an intervener early on and never knew it."

Adam looked back at Delilah and then looked at me. "Have I told you thank you, Mrs. H, for everything you've done for us?"

"No need for thanks, dear. This is what I was born to do. So, how is your law firm doing, Adam?"

"I guess kind of slow lately. Hopefully, it will pick up.

Why do you ask?" Adam asked curiously.

"The school is always in need of vocational teachers. Oh, never mind me. I'm just thinking aloud."

Adam, a teacher and an advocate for the deaf and blind. Hmm … wouldn't that be something.

~ ADAM ~

We arrived at the Liberty School for the Blind, and I have to admit that I was a bit nervous. Kate used to volunteer many hours here, but I had never ventured out to visit the school. Having found out that Mrs. Hamilton's sons worked there had truly aroused my curiosity. It made me wonder what Delilah's life would be like.

We pulled up to a large campus with many buildings spread throughout the plush green lawns. It was a beautiful setting with lots of trees and flowers. Paved paths throughout the landscape made me think that the students were able to maneuver with ease. It appeared that the paths intertwined and had points of interest that helped students walk along the paths. I noticed a statue of a little girl with her dog at the end of one path. I realized that with each different statue, bench, or fountain, a student would be able to tell where he or she was. It was sort of like the stations we had set up at home for Delilah.

I was lost in my thoughts as I sat taking it all in. Mrs. Hamilton touched my arm and asked, "Adam, are you okay?

I guess you didn't hear me. The campus is glorious, isn't it?"

"It is truly beautiful. Nothing like I had in my mind."

"You will be even more thrilled once we step inside. Liberty School is one of a kind."

We parked the car, pulled Delilah's stroller out of the back, and placed her in the stroller with her sippy cup and caterpillar. This was one of those times when I wished that she could see the beauty all around. We walked up to the big wooden doors and pulled a chain hanging from the door. I wanted to ask about it but thought I would just go with the flow. Shortly, a young woman of about sixteen answered the door. She smiled and motioned us in.

I couldn't stand it anymore. "Okay, Mrs. H, can you explain about the chain on the door?"

"When the chain is pulled, it triggers a light that comes on for the young woman at the desk. She knows someone is at the door. Her job is greeter and receptionist. She can also answer the phone by using a Video Relay Service, which is a free service for the deaf. It helps her receive and send calls to and from students, family members, or people interested in the school. A certified ASL interpreter is on one end of the Service to help her use the Internet connection. It is truly remarkable. The greeter is not blind, but she is deaf. The jobs on this campus vary depending on the need. Rest assured that they find something where every student can be productive and take pride in his or her work. It won't be long before a deaf and blind person will share this job. The training is a bit more extensive, but it is possible."

We started walking down a long hall. The school was buzzing with action. Young and old alike were moving about in the halls. I saw two young men having an in-depth conversation to my right. A little farther was a young girl, maybe five years old, walking with her cane without assistance. All of a sudden, I heard a voice behind us.

"Mrs. Hamilton, welcome, welcome. I see you've brought some of your friends to visit today. Have you seen Brandon and Michael yet?"

"Adam, let me introduce you to Mr. Smith. He is a dear old friend who has been here as long as I have," Mrs. Hamilton said with a smile.

"Nice to meet you, Mr. Smith."

"Well, the same here, Adam," said Mr. Smith looking down at Delilah. "I know this little angel. She has been here many times with her mother. Oh, please forgive me, Adam. I'm so sorry for your loss."

"Thank you. It hasn't been easy for us. We miss her very much."

"You know, Adam, I have a picture of Kate and Delilah on the bulletin board in my office. It was taken at our last Valentine's Day party. I'd like you to have it."

"Thank you. I would appreciate that."

"Harvey, we have to be moving along now, but we will stop by on our way out," said Mrs. Hamilton.

"That would be wonderful. It was nice meeting you,

Adam. Bye for now," said Mr. Smith as he walked away.

Just about that time, Mrs. Hamilton looked up to see her son Michael walking down the hall with a beautiful black lab and a young boy. She walked up to Michael, placed her hand in his palm, and began signing. He smiled broadly and gave his mom a big hug. Then Michael leaned down, placed his fingers on the inside of the boy's palm, and signed something. The young boy turned and headed back in the opposite direction.

Mrs. Hamilton and Michael began signing back and forth. Michael reached his hand out to shake mine.

"Adam, this is my son Michael and his dog Toby that goes everywhere with him. We're going to walk down to Delilah's room with Michael. This is where she will attend school and where Kate used to bring her. Brandon works with Delilah's age group, so he'll be working with her on a daily basis."

We walked down the hall and turned to the left into a large, open room filled with many students and interpreters. The children, who were Delilah's age and a bit older, were busy working on many different tasks. Mrs. Hamilton interrupted Brandon, who was sitting with a young girl of about five. Mrs. Hamilton tapped Brandon's shoulder gently, took his hand, and signed. Like Michael, Brandon stood up and hugged his mother. She introduced us, and like his brother, he put his hand out for me to shake. It was then that I wanted to know sign language so badly. I could carry on a conversation with these men if I knew how to sign. My goal would be to learn sign language as fast as I could.

Mrs. Hamilton placed Delilah in a chair, and Brandon came near her. He reached out, took her little hand, and made the sign for hello. Delilah didn't move. She quietly sat there, which I thought was peculiar. She still had her caterpillar in her other arm, holding it tightly.

"It will be a wonderful thing to see Delilah grow in this environment, Adam. In time, you'll see your little girl blossom," said Mrs. Hamilton, who was signing to Brandon as she spoke to me. Brandon then signed back to his mom, and Mrs. Hamilton relayed his message. "Adam, I'm happy to meet you. Mom has told us all about you and Delilah. I promise I will do everything I can to open the world up for Delilah."

I looked at Mrs. Hamilton and asked her to sign thank you for me. Instead of signing it, she said to me, "Here, you try." She took my hand, showed me the sign for thank you, and then placed my fingers on Brandon's open palm. I signed thank you, and he smiled and nodded his head.

We stayed for a couple of hours watching the teachers, interpreters, Michael, and Brandon work around the room. It was the most fascinating environment I have ever seen. It was time to go, and we said our goodbyes. I had learned how to sign hello, goodbye, and thank you. It was truly a good day. Brandon reached down and once again signed into Delilah's palm, goodbye. Then she reached for Brandon's hand and signed hello. It truly was a good day.

We walked to Mr. Smith's office, and as he had promised, he handed me the picture of Kate and Delilah. Kate was wearing a white shirt with pink hearts all over it. Delilah was wearing a matching shirt with hearts all over it, too. Kate was kissing Delilah on the cheek, and Delilah was smiling broadly. I could feel the tears begin to fall and could barely whisper, "Thank you."

I realized that day that Delilah had a really good chance of making something out of her life. Her disabilities would never define her.

Chapter Nine

The Cochlear Implants

~ ADAM ~

I put all my appointments that today on hold because Delilah and I had an important meeting. There have been many twists and turns this past year, but they have all been good. Delilah has been at Liberty School for the Blind for the last three years. She has mastered sign language, and that is quite an accomplishment for one so young. She is using a walking cane and signing. And the academic testing has identified that she is quite gifted. As her father, I had no doubt.

I have also become proficient in sign language. It is wonderful to be able to communicate with Delilah. It has been a long road for both of us. But once the light went on, there was no stopping this father and daughter team.

I had received a call earlier that day that let me know the speech pathologist would meet with us. Mrs. Hamilton has been talking to me about Delilah getting cochlear implants. I haven't pursued it for a couple of reasons. First, we don't qualify for any help through the government. Delilah's school is very costly. It has taken all the money I could muster to keep her there. In these last three years, I have used up all of the small life insurance policy that Kate left for Delilah. The second problem is that I have my own business, and I don't have medical insurance. The procedure is very costly. I believe it is more important for Delilah to get as much therapy as possible while I am able to pay for it. Recently, however, I found out about a grant through the school that helps three students a year with the cost of cochlear implants.

I picked up Delilah early from class, and we headed to our appointment across the campus. We walked into the office and had barely sat down when a young woman came out to greet us.

"Hello, my name is Julie Simms. You must be Adam and Delilah. Please come in."

"Yes. I'll be honest, Ms. Simms. I'm not sure about this at all."

"Adam, when I received the referral and saw that Delilah was one of the three to receive the grant, I had to get you in as soon as possible. Delilah is so far ahead of most of our students. I wanted to speak to you about cochlear implants for Delilah because she is already six. Are you familiar with this hearing device?" asked Ms. Simms.

"Of course, I am, Ms. Simms. But honestly, I'm not sure if this is something that Delilah would benefit from. I don't want to go through the whole process only for her to be disappointed."

Ms. Simms looked at me with a very serious look. "I understand what your concerns are. Sometimes the children have great results, but it's a long road of speech therapy and hearing therapy after the implants. Honestly, sometimes it's many years. If she is able to hear sounds with the implants, it may be possible for Delilah to speak one day."

"Ms. Simms, I have watched my little girl learn to communicate. She's happy and content. I don't know if I want her to go through this. It may be a lot of wasted time. And I would rather that she succeed in learning more productive tasks such as math, reading, and learning to be just a kid. I've also read that it is not always successful and can be very stressful."

There was a knock on the door. I turned around to see Mrs. Hamilton.

"I hope you don't mind, Adam. I thought Ms. Simms might be able to explain this better than I could. I've wished many times that these implants could have been available back when my boys were young. Now they don't want to bother with them. The implants might have made a difference for my boys. Adam, I don't want to tell you what to do, but I'm afraid Delilah is outgrowing our program so fast that she may have to attend public school as her needs become less. I've heard a rumor that the school may be closing in the next couple of years since state funding will be cut drastically. I love Delilah, and I want her to be able to get all the help she needs while there's time. With cochlear implants, she'll be able to get intense therapy and maybe even learn to speak. We're one of the few schools that work with deaf and blind children."

I sat there looking at Delilah and thinking that this was such a difficult decision. Why is it so hard? Maybe part of me was scared. We have just now adjusted to the non-hearing world. Even though Delilah was only six, I wanted to know what she thought about this. She was mature for her years. I was amazed how grown-up she appeared for six years of age. If she could talk, I was sure she would sound like a little woman. I saw many of Kate's mannerisms in her.

I signed to Delilah about our conversation and about the cochlear implants. Her eyes got big. She took my hand and signed, "Pop, I want to learn to talk. Please, Pop, I want to hear!"

I looked at Mrs. Hamilton who was standing in the back of the room wiping her eyes. Then I looked at Ms. Simms and back at Delilah. I took Delilah's hand and signed, "Are you sure?"

Delilah took my hand and signed back, "I love you, Pop. I want to say it with words one day."

I signed back to her, "You already have."

Once the decision had been made, I had a feeling our

whole world was going to change. One of the things I had read was that the deaf community was just that: a community. I had my concerns. Would Delilah still be a part of the community? Would they still accept her, knowing that she could hear? Caught between two worlds—the hearing world and the non-hearing world—would Delilah be able to handle this?

Chapter Ten
The Test Results

~ ADAM ~

*I*t had been six weeks since Delilah had the surgery to put in the cochlear devices. She had to stay in the hospital for a couple of days, and I stayed by her bedside. Delilah, Mrs. Hamilton, and I sat in the doctor's office waiting for the testing to determine the effectiveness of the implants and whether Delilah would be able to hear.

We had followed prescribed steps to even get to that point. I couldn't imagine going through this without being able to communicate the steps along the way to Delilah, but she had been a real trooper.

We were referred to an otolaryngologist—an ear, nose, and throat specialist—a couple of weeks prior to surgery. They wanted to make sure that this was a good idea for Delilah. An audiologist tested her hearing and once again found that Delilah had profound deafness in both ears. The speech pathologist tested Delilah's language skills and found that she had no verbal skills. That would take many years of follow-up speech and hearing therapy.

Cleared to schedule the surgery, we went to a pre-op appointment, during which the otolaryngologist checked to make sure that Delilah was healthy enough to have the surgery. We had already met with Ms. Simms at the school to discuss the future of Delilah's speech and hearing therapy.

On the day of the surgery, I had been nervous. Delilah had to reassure me that she would be okay. The operation took about three hours. They had explained to me that a small cut would be made behind the ear so that they could get to the inner ear. The electrodes would be connected to the cochlea. The wires and transmitter would be connected to the bone. It would take about six weeks for her to heal.

On the day that the implants would be turned on for the first time, Delilah, Mrs. Hamilton, and I were sitting there waiting for the doctor. Delilah was more anxious than normal. She was sitting in the chair, patting her hands nervously on the sides of the chair. I took her hands and held them in mine. I stroked her cheek.

"Delilah, are you excited about this day?" I signed to her.

"I am so happy, Pop. I want to learn to sing, but I am scared, too!"

I couldn't help but smile at the thought of Delilah singing. I signed back to her, "Really, what makes singing so special to you?"

"You told me that when I was a baby, you and Momma would dance with me, and I would fall asleep. I want to hear the music, Pop!"

Suddenly, tears filled my eyes. I know that Kate is looking down upon us with a big smile right now. Oh, how I wish she could be sharing this moment with us.

"Pop, you seem upset. Your hands are trembling," signed Delilah into my hands. Delilah reached to my face and felt the wet tears there. Her smile suddenly turned to a frown. "Oh, Pop, why are you crying?" signed Delilah.

"Oh, these things?" I placed her hand on my cheek to feel the tears. "They are just tears of joy, my love. Just tears of happiness," I signed back to Delilah.

Mrs. Hamilton took Delilah's hands in hers and started signing, "I have a special gift for you once we get home."

"Oh, please tell me what it is, GG," signed Delilah.

Delilah had called Mrs. Hamilton "GG" since the day she started working with her. It was actually Kate's idea. "Mrs. Hamilton" was difficult to sign at Delilah's young age. Kate felt it wasn't proper for Delilah to call her teacher by her first name, and Kate used to tell Mrs. Hamilton what a "Great Gift" she was to Delilah. Thus, "GG" was born.

"It is a surprise, but I am sure you will love it," signed Mrs. Hamilton.

Then the nurse called our names to take us to the doctor's office. Dr. Ellingsworth greeted us with a smile and asked us to sit down.

"Are you ready for the big day, Delilah?" the doctor signed into Delilah's hand.

Since Delilah was already nervous, she could only nod her head yes and clasp her hands tightly together.

"The first thing we are going to do is connect everything. I will turn on the device and use the lowest frequency until we see if Delilah responds," explained the doctor.

Dr. Ellingsworth signed to Delilah, "Delilah, I need you to raise your hand or tap my arm if you hear anything at any time. Okay?" Delilah once more nodded yes.

We watched as the doctor connected everything. With great anticipation, we held our breaths as he turned on the device. Each time he raised the threshold of frequency higher, our hearts beat faster until, suddenly, Delilah raised her little hand, stood up quickly, and jumped up and down! Signing at record speed into each of our hands, she began to cry tears of joy. There was no stopping her. She had heard something, and her excitement couldn't be contained.

Mrs. Hamilton grabbed me, planted the biggest kiss on my cheek, and hugged me with a bear hug. I could hardly breathe. I felt like screaming at the top of my lungs, "My daughter can hear!" But I tried to maintain some kind of sanity among the excitement.

"This is wonderful," said Dr. Ellingsworth. "Delilah can hear about middle range. While she still has significant loss, I believe this is a good sign. Next, I will test the higher frequencies and see what is comfortable for her," explained the doctor.

Delilah was so excited that she couldn't sit down. I was sitting there in a stupor. I was in shock! Mrs. Hamilton had to step in to calm the situation down and bring us both back to reality.

"Dear heart," Mrs. Hamilton signed to Delilah, "the doctor has some more testing to do. Sit by me so he can finish the test."

"Adam, are you all right?" Mrs. Hamilton asked me.

"I think so. I'm speechless right now."

"Are we ready?" asked Dr. Ellingsworth, smiling.

He began the second round of testing, and it seemed as if he were turning it higher and higher. I was worried, thinking maybe this was not going to work. All of a sudden, Delilah started hitting the doctor's arm and nodding yes.

"Excellent job, Delilah," said the doctor. "Excellent! Now I will store these readings into the computer, which will draw a map *per se* and then present sounds to Delilah. I'm not sure if these sounds will scare her, or possibly make her cry, or if she will even respond. We can only watch her reactions."

The doctor turned to Delilah and signed, "Delilah, like before, I am going to give you some sounds to hear. They may sound scary or different, but we need to see if you can hear them," explained Dr. Ellingsworth.

The doctor began to test the new sounds, and we could tell by Delilah's expressions that she was hearing sounds.

Her eyes were wide open, and she kept nodding yes. She squeezed my hand tightly and then grabbed Mrs. Hamilton's hands. With us on both sides of Delilah, she sat nodding and squeezing for the next twenty minutes.

"Okay, we're done!" explained Dr. Ellingsworth. "I would say that the implants appear to be a great success. Of course, you know you will have many years ahead for Delilah to learn to speak, but I do believe you did this at just the right time. Over the next few weeks, I will see Delilah back here, since I'm sure there will be some adjustments that will need to be made. I would say after that, if all goes well, I might see her three or four times the first year."

We all hugged the doctor, and Delilah signed, "Thank you."

"You are so welcome, Delilah," signed Dr. Ellingsworth back to her.

We left the doctor's office smiling, with our hearts so full. We had just received a miracle! Kate, are you smiling, my love?

When we returned home, Mrs. Hamilton pulled out a brightly colored gift box. She placed it in Delilah's hands and signed to Delilah, "I have been saving this for a special day such as this. While you will not understand the noise coming from it today, one day you will. It is a music box, my dear. I want you to have this. It belonged to me when I was a little girl."

Mrs. Hamilton turned the key, and Delilah opened the

lid slowly. Delilah turned her head curiously because she could hear sounds. Though they may not have sounded like music just yet, she knew that they were sounds.

"I can hear sounds!" Delilah signed to Mrs. Hamilton. "Please tell me what song it is playing."

Mrs. Hamilton signed, "It is called 'Somewhere Over the Rainbow.' It is a song about following your dreams and about dreams coming true."

Delilah signed back to Mrs. Hamilton, "My dreams are coming true, GG."

"Yes, they are, my dear. Yes, they are," said Mrs. Hamilton as she signed back to Delilah.

Chapter Eleven

Graduation Day

~ ADAM ~

I yelled to Delilah nervously, "Hurry, Delilah. We're going to be late! I'm sure your hair looks beautiful." I attempted to adjust my tie for the hundredth time. Kate would have had this tied in no time.

"Pop, you know these curls and I battle. Why did I have to have this mound of hair anyway?" Delilah asked, laughing and signing so quickly that she was making me nervous. Delilah speaks very well and is very articulate, but she still signs as she speaks. I'm happy that the therapist has allowed her to do this. I had heard that sometimes therapists discourage it. But Delilah told them she always wants to use her hands to speak, too. She doesn't do this for herself, but for others. She says that we never know who may be around who cannot hear or see.

"It's not like I can see it, but I can feel it, and it's a mess, isn't it, Pop?" Delilah asked, slightly frustrated from a bad case of nerves.

"No, it is not!" I argued playfully. "Leave it down. Let it have its way. You look beautiful, just like your mother."

"Daddy," Delilah signed, "do you think Mom sees us today?" When Delilah signed Daddy, I always knew she was thinking about Kate. She would become that little girl who longed for her mother.

"I have no doubt, honey. Your mom has always been our guardian angel," I responded.

This was a special day. My Delilah was graduating from high school. Not only was she graduating from high school, she was also giving the class speech. As I looked back on how we got here, I was amazed all over again.

Thirteen years had passed since Delilah received her cochlear implants. The world had been opened to her as one big gift. She started receiving hearing and speech therapy right away. We worked for years to get to where we are today.

Delilah's blindness had never been her thorn. But not to be able to see or hear had been really hard for her. She told me she felt captive inside her body. Delilah explained that she had feelings and thoughts like everyone else but couldn't always communicate them.

Every day had been a new learning experience for both of us. Every opportunity we had, we took advantage of what was before us. Because we looked at life as a big classroom, I believe it helped Delilah learn to talk sooner than most who have received cochlear implants. Every day had been an open book, and we anticipated new adventures to be shared and experienced.

Music therapy had been the first type of therapy used. Kate always used music to help calm Delilah when she was a baby. Delilah felt the movement when Kate danced with her. It had been familiar in many ways when Delilah first heard music. She put the puzzle together when she was introduced to sounds. After that happened, Delilah learned to play the piano and became quite the musician. She would sit and practice for hours on the piano. Mrs. Hamilton played the piano and was the perfect person to teach Delilah how to play. Sometimes Mrs. Hamilton had to tell Delilah that she was tired because Delilah would spend hours at the keys.

I had attempted to do my part as well, playing music and dancing with Delilah. It was easy for me to dream of the day when I would take her in my arms as we danced the father and daughter dance at her wedding. There was nothing that could stop Delilah. I also sang to her, and she would end up laughing and begging me to stop. I had to admit I was not a great singer.

Then came the years of hearing and speech therapy, but it had been worth every minute. She had some of the best teachers. When Delilah was ten, the school did close, as Mrs. Hamilton had predicted. Oh, that was such a sad day. Mrs. Hamilton retired but continued to work with Delilah. Brandon and Michael also pitched in their time until they moved to another school in the state. There they continued to offer their expertise and to help teach many students.

Ms. Simms became very special to us. She worked with Delilah at Halstead High School, the public school Delilah started attending. Delilah never allowed her disabilities keep her from doing the things she loved. She played the piano and had public-speaking engagements for teacher workshops during the summers. Between Ms. Simms and me, we traveled with Delilah. I can't tell you how much fan mail that Delilah received on a daily basis. Delilah decided to be a public speaker and to travel to all areas of the nation to tell her story. She wanted to be a representative for the deaf and blind.

I decided to do some work on the legal aspects for people who have disabilities. I help them fight for their right to better services within the schools and the communities. I represented a young man named Daniel who couldn't access a public library due to no ramps. He was wheelchair bound. The town didn't feel they had to move quickly on this situation. It had been over a year since Daniel's petition had begun. The town mayor said they didn't have the funds to make every public facility accessible to wheelchairs. However, they had money to hold their yearly state fair, and the city footed the entire bill. I met Daniel at one of Delilah's public-speaking engagements. Delilah and Daniel became quite good friends.

Delilah and I headed for the stadium. Delilah was

wearing her mother's pearls, her black mortarboard, and her gown. Her red hair's lovely curls were past her shoulders. She was a natural beauty with a few freckles sprinkled across her button nose. She was about five feet four and petite. She looked so much like Kate.

I remembered one time when Delilah asked me what she looked like. She was about eight at the time. I pulled her near me and started from the top of her head and went all the way down to the tips of her toes. She couldn't comprehend colors or outward beauty. Delilah's beauty is expressed in music. So, I told her that she is as lovely as the music she plays.

Mrs. Hamilton slid in next to Ms. Simms and me. Delilah was already on stage sitting with the other speakers. I had butterflies in my stomach.

"Did you bring tissues, Adam?" Mrs. Hamilton asked.

Patting my shirt pocket, I said, "Yep, right here."

Mrs. Hamilton leaned over to Ms. Simms, "Hello, dear. Nice to see you," giving me a little wink. I knew what she was thinking.

Daniel wheeled up beside the row of chairs.

"Hello, Daniel. It's good to see you!" I said, extending my hand with a friendly smile.

"I wouldn't miss this for the world," Daniel grinned.

"Here they are, Eddie. Hi, ya'll," said Beth, pushing her way over our legs to claim the empty chairs beside Mrs. Hamilton. "Come on, Eddie," yelled Beth.

Eddie quickly followed behind, noticeably flustered, but

still managing a quick hello. "Women!" he whispered.

I looked down the row, noting our family. There was Mrs. H, Ms. Simms, Daniel, Eddie, and Beth. Just as I thought we had finished filling up the row, I heard, "Adam, you didn't think we would miss our girl's graduation, did you?" I looked up to see Ben, Mia, and the twins. What a great surprise! Details must have been worked out after all because Ben hadn't been sure he could get off work, or if the boys could be released from school early. I couldn't have been more thrilled.

"We're not late, are we?" Ben asked. I smiled, shook hands with Ben, and gave Mia a quick kiss on the cheek.

"It's about to start. You're just in time," I replied.

The chairs quickly filled, and the happy families started to settle down. Mr. Brown, the school superintendent, made his way to the podium.

"Good afternoon, and thank you for honoring our students on their very special day. I would like to introduce you to a young woman who has won all of our hearts. She is the picture of success. I will not say much more about her. Please welcome Delilah Moore."

I could hear cheering all around, and I felt my heart beating out of my chest. Our whole family stood, yelled, clapped, whistled, and shouted, with Beth leading the way. We couldn't stop and couldn't have been more proud. We finally settled down, and that's when we realized all eyes were on us, but we didn't care.

There, standing in front of several thousand people, was my Delilah. All of a sudden, a hush settled over the crowd as Delilah began to speak.

"Dear fellow students, faculty, family members, and friends.

"I stand before you with much love and gratitude in my heart. I would like to share with you about my life. I was born both deaf and blind. I was born into a body that did not work like many of your bodies. It held me captive. I wanted to communicate, but I could not. I learned sign language at a very young age, and it helped me communicate. Then, at the age of six, I received my cochlear implants, which helped me to hear so that I could learn to talk with my voice. My parents, along with the aid of some wonderful people, helped me grow into the person I am today by believing in me. I will always be a part of the deaf community. I have devices that help me hear, but I am still deaf without them. I cannot and will not forget who I am.

"My parents are the best. They always made me feel like I was just like other children and that I could do anything I put my mind to do. My mom passed away when I was almost three years old, but she has always been with me in spirit. I have felt her presence every day. Both of my parents sacrificed so much time, money, and energy helping me to become the person I am today. Mrs. Hamilton, my "GG," gave of herself to help teach us since I was a baby. She has become like a loving grandmother to me.

"Thanks to the help of some wonderfully supportive people, I have been able to learn to speak and hear after six years of living in total silence. If I can overcome those obstacles, then you, my classmates, can go out into the world and climb mountains. Never forget where you have come from. Stay true to yourself. Never try to be something or someone you are not.

"I want to leave you with this one last thought. We are all born deaf and blind until life touches us. We are born knowing nothing. It is up to us to make our lives the best they can be, to work hard, to continue to learn, and not to take one day for granted. Each of us needs to treat our life as if it is the best gift we have ever received.

"Pop, I love you. Thank you, Momma. Thank you, Mrs. Hamilton and Ms. Simms. I love you all. Thank you."

Delilah received a standing ovation, and there was not a dry eye in the house. Then Delilah moved from the podium and made her way, with the help of one of her beloved teachers, to the piano that sat at the end of the stage. She sat down and played one of her favorite songs, "Somewhere Over the Rainbow." As Delilah hit the last key, she blew a kiss into the air. I knew Kate was there catching it in her hands.

Chapter Twelve
The Wedding

~ DELILAH ~

*L*ying dreamily in the bed I now shared with Daniel, I thought about our wedding ceremony and our wedding night. They were everything I had ever dreamed they could be.

Daniel was up early. I could hear him whistling in the bathroom. He had heard Pop cleaning up and told me he should offer to help. I told him I would be waiting for him to come back to bed. He smiled, kissed me, and hurried out the door to help Pop clean up after the wedding.

I lay there thinking about the last four years and our wedding last night. I was now a married woman. Twirling the ring on my finger, I remembered thinking that I never would get married. I wasn't sure if anyone would want to marry me. Pop always said I was silly to think that way. He always said I would be a catch for the right man, but that man would have to pass Pop's test. Smiling to myself, I guessed that Daniel must have passed the test.

Like many young people, I had attended college filled with many hopes and dreams. I had decided to become a teacher, a public speaker, and an advocate for deaf and blind people in this world. Pop had been a nervous wreck when he found out I wanted to live in the dorms. I had Daniel, so I wasn't afraid. Daniel had been in college for two years prior to my starting there, and we had met through my dad.

Actually, Daniel had shown up at one of my public speaking engagements the summer before my senior year of high school. He managed to meet my dad there, and they had instantly liked one another. Daniel told my dad about some problems he had been having with the city concerning the construction of wheelchair-accessible ramps into the local library. My dad had already started to do some *pro bono* work for other people with disabilities, so he was glad to help Daniel. Dad and Daniel spent many days working on their case to convince the city to build wheelchair ramps at the local library. You would have thought they were trying to introduce a new law into congress. It was just that difficult. They did win their case in the end, and the city built the ramps. I never suspected I would fall in love so young, but I had always been a bit more mature than most girls my age.

I really enjoyed the early mornings. I would sit outside and feel the sunshine on my face. My hearing was such a gift, and I never forgot that, at one time, I couldn't hear even one sound. I found those mornings to be the most precious times. I could hear the birds chirping, and it was music to my ears. Daniel started showing up quite often it seemed, making some excuse to see my dad. Then he would make his way outside, bringing me a cream-filled donut and coffee. We would sit and talk for a couple of hours. That summer passed quickly. Daniel started back to college, and I began my senior year. Our friendship began to grow before we knew it.

Daniel was not born with disabilities. He had been in a car accident when he was sixteen that left him paralyzed on the left side. He was able to drive, and he could transfer himself into and out of his wheelchair. If he took his time, he could walk with a cane. He had been awarded a rather large settlement after the accident that paid for college. He believed that he would walk again one day. I believed that, too.

We laughed and made jokes about our relationship. "What a fine pair we are!" he said. We never talked about what we couldn't do. Instead, we talked about what we could do. Luckily, we both were stubborn enough to make our relationship work.

I will never forget the day I knew I had fallen in love with Daniel. He had come by in the morning, but it was raining. I was sitting in the kitchen reading. He wheeled in and said his usual, "Good morning, Sunshine!"

"Well, not today, I'm afraid," I said with a laugh. "It's raining hard out there." Daniel wheeled next to me, rather close, and I could feel the warmth of his body near me. He smelled like musk. His breath smelled sweet. I felt tingling going through my whole body. I had never felt that before. I could feel him lean over to look at my book, and then it happened. I leaned over, touched his face, and kissed him. It was not just a peck on the cheek but a deep, loving kiss on his lips. After that kiss, there was no going back. We kissed often that year, and we still do. I knew I loved him. After that first kiss, we knew we were going to be together for a long time. Our future together was not a question of how. It was just a question of when.

Daniel was with me during my college days and accepted the job as my personal caregiver. Pop didn't even ask him. Daniel told Pop that he was going to take care of me at college, so Pop didn't have to worry. I told Daniel that this was too much to ask of anyone, but he wouldn't have it any other way. Daniel majored in law, and of course, my dad thought Daniel was the best.

During four years of college, we had stressful days, but many were wonderful, too. Daniel had to make sure that his classes wouldn't interfere with mine. We constantly were juggling our schedules. I look back and have no idea how we did it.

Daniel was in law school during my senior year of college. Our plans were to get married after he graduated and found a job. Pop had already decided that he wanted Daniel to work for him if Daniel agreed. Daniel graduated in January and started working for Pop right away.

The closer our wedding date came, the more nervous I got. Sometimes, I would get a little down, since I'm only human. I began to doubt whether Daniel should have this responsibility. Was I asking too much of him to marry a blind woman? He got really angry with me when I asked him. He looked at me and asked, "Am I asking too much of you to marry someone who cannot walk?"

"Of course not," I declared, with fire in my eyes. Then the subject would be dropped until the next time it resurfaced. I guess we both understood that getting married was a serious step.

Pop said we could live with him since he was going to be out of town a lot, and the house would just sit unoccupied. With Daniel and Pop working together, it would make things easier. We knew the area well. It was familiar, which was the best thing for us then. Pop was great in that he knew we needed our privacy. He had given up the bottom floor and had moved to the spare room upstairs. He knew that with Daniel's wheelchair, the ground floor would be the better choice for us. Our room was right next to the kitchen, and it had its own bath. The kitchen led out into the living room. I could get around perfectly. I had grown up in this house, and Pop hadn't moved one thing.

I wanted to have our wedding here at the house. Beth and GG helped by decorating the house. Daniel, Pop, and Eddie picked up the chairs and tables. Having the wedding in June was the perfect time of year in San Francisco. I had left all of the wedding details up to the ladies, but I picked out the perfect song, "Always and Forever."

Pictures were taken, but Pop and Daniel were my eyes. Pop talked me through coming down the stairs and walking down the aisle, and then Daniel talked me through the ceremony, describing every detail from top to bottom.

I knew that the colors were baby blue and white, that there were carnations, and that candles had been lit for the evening wedding. Beth and GG explained every detail to me. The details really didn't matter to me. All I could think about was that I was going to be Daniel's wife. Daniel attempted to explain the color blue to me, but I had never seen the sky. I knew that the sky was blue, but I couldn't picture it. He said baby blue was soft like his gentle touch, like a lullaby that I played on the piano. It was quiet and peaceful. Then I could feel the color blue. Daniel was the only one who could take something I had never seen and describe it in a way that I would understand. Pop could do that, too, but Daniel had a gift, a way of making the world that he described come alive for me.

Ben's wife, Mia, selected my dress for me. That was something she wanted to do. I wanted something simple. Mia asked me what I was thinking. I told her that when I touched it, I didn't want to feel any beads, lace, or frills. I wanted my dress to feel smooth to the touch. She chose a simple white dress made from silk that had been specially made in Japan. Mia explained white in this way. She said it was like the beginning of time or the feeling when you start something new. She said it was like holding a fresh rose in your hand. The petals were soft and had perfect lines without any ridges or blemishes. White was pureness. It was a symbol for virginity. It was a young woman who had not known another. I knew white. I could feel the color white. It was Daniel's love, pure and simple, for me. Daniel and I would become one for the first time. My dress represented this union.

Beth and GG helped me get ready in the upstairs bedroom. Beth explained that she had put my hair up in a French twist with small, delicate white and blue flowers. She placed a pearl necklace that had belonged to her mother around my neck. GG put a simple diamond bracelet that had belonged to my mother around my wrist. My bouquet was placed in my hands, and Pop got ready to escort me down the stairs.

He took my arm, put his arm around it, and placed his hand on top of mine. We began to walk. "You look beautiful, Delilah. You look just like your mother."

"Thank you, Daddy," I said.

"You haven't called me 'Daddy' in a very long time," he said as he squeezed my hand. "I've missed it."

Pop began to tell me what he saw as we walked down the upstairs hall. I could hear the music playing in the background.

"Delilah, the house looks beautiful. The stairs are decorated with blue and white flowers along the banister."

We started to step down the stairs slowly.

"All of your family is watching you come down the stairs, and they are smiling. I see Ben, Mia, and the twins. They are standing looking at you. Ben is wiping his eyes. Mrs. H is wearing her large purple flower, but she is also wearing a large purple hat." I giggled at the thought of Mrs. H's flower and hat.

Pop continued, "Eddie and Beth are arm in arm, like two proud parents, watching your every step."

"Pop, and Daniel? Where is Daniel?" I asked nervously.

Adam looked toward the man his daughter loved, the man who would soon be his son-in-law. Daniel had confided earlier that he wanted to stand beside his bride during the ceremony. Adam smiled as Daniel rose from his wheelchair with determination and might, using his cane for support. He stood tall as he watched his beautiful bride make her way toward him.

"Daniel is standing by the minister. He is wearing a black suit. Black as the darkness you see every day, but his shirt is white with a baby blue tie. Large candles are lit everywhere, making the room look like a sunset. Do you remember the song *Evergreen* by Barbra Streisand that you play on the piano? It looks like that song." I smiled because I love that song. "It is my light in the darkness," I had explained to Pop.

"I am going to place your hand in Daniel's hand, and then the ceremony will begin," said Pop as he reluctantly released my hand into Daniel's.

I could hear a sniff come from Pop, like maybe he was crying. "Pop, are you okay?" I asked as I reached up and wiped a tear from his cheek. "I love you, Daddy. I really do," I told him.

"I know you do. And I love you. Now go, be happy," Pop said, as he gave me away.

Chapter Thirteen
Coming Full Circle

A sudden wave of nausea engulfed Delilah. She rolled to the edge of the bed, thinking she may have to jump out in a hurry. "Are you okay, Delilah?" Daniel asked.

"I feel sick to my stomach, Daniel. Maybe I have a bug or something. I have a speaking engagement today, and I can't miss it!" she explained to Daniel.

Daniel and Delilah had been married for two years, and life could not have been better. They were genuinely happy. Delilah got up, took a shower, and started to dress. All of a sudden, she felt herself falling and was barely able to yell out for Daniel.

"Delilah! Delilah!" Daniel screamed, attempting to awaken Delilah, who was lying on the bathroom floor. She did not respond.

Daniel grabbed the phone and called 9-1-1. He ran to the door and yelled for Adam, who was upstairs. Then Daniel covered Delilah's body to keep her warm.

Adam came running into the bathroom and knelt beside Delilah. "Honey, wake up. Baby, it's Daddy. Wake up."

Delilah began to open her eyes. Realizing that something had happened, she yelled for Daniel.

"We're here, sweetheart. Daniel is here, too," said Adam, trying to console her.

"What happened?" Delilah asked.

"I think you fainted," Daniel said, moving her hair gently from her eyes.

The EMS crew arrived and transported Delilah to the hospital emergency room. Daniel and Adam stood anxiously by her side.

It seemed like hours had passed as Daniel and Adam waited for the doctor to tell them something. Finally, the doctor came into the room and addressed Delilah, Adam, and Daniel.

"Well, I believe we've found out what may have caused Delilah to faint. And I am happy to say it is something that will correct itself in time," said the doctor with a smile.

All eyes were on the doctor as he delivered the news. "Congratulations, Delilah, you're going to have a baby!"

Daniel's mouth fell open as he stared at the doctor. Adam looked at Delilah in shock.

Delilah lay there in total silence. Her mind was reeling.

A baby! We have never even thought about a baby. I mean our careers have been our focus. I am on birth control. How did this happen? Are we equipped to raise a child? Is it fair to have a child with our disabilities?

Daniel wheeled his way around the bed and took Delilah's hands. "Baby, we're going to have a baby!" Delilah could feel the happiness in Daniel's voice.

"Daddy, are you there?"

"I'm here. It's wonderful news, Delilah. Really. Don't worry. It's going to be okay," Adam reassured her.

Delilah's mind continued to whirl. *Of course, everyone is thinking the same thing but not saying a word. How is this going to work? What if the baby is born with the same disabilities I have? How could I care for her or him? How can I care for my baby?* There were so many concerns.

The doctor told Delilah to make her first prenatal appointment right away. He said that she needed to make sure she ate several small meals a day. He thought she fainted because her blood sugar got too low. He gave her strict orders to rest for the next couple of days.

That night as Daniel held Delilah in his arms in their bed, he attempted to reassure her. "Delilah, we will hire a nanny to help you. Please don't worry. This baby is meant to be a gift."

Delilah turned over toward Daniel, resting her head on his chest. "What if he or she is born the way I was?"

"You mean amazing, beautiful, smart, and absolutely

wonderful in every way?" Daniel asked and held her tighter. "Delilah, we'll take one day at a time. There is nothing we cannot do, together." At that very moment, Delilah believed Daniel with all her heart.

Pop had been very quiet lately, and Delilah could tell that something was on his mind. She finally found a few minutes of time alone with him.

"Pop, can you sit with me a few minutes, so we can talk?" He thought it sounded like a little girl's plea.

"Of course," he replied. "I always have time for my beautiful little girl."

"What do you think about the baby? I mean, you really have not said very much."

Delilah could tell she had really hit a nerve. Something wasn't right, and her Pop wasn't himself.

"Delilah, there's something you don't know about your old man, and I don't know if I should even tell you. It happened so long ago, and I have tried to make up for my stupidity. But I'm not proud of something I did."

"Pop, there's nothing you could tell me that would make me love you less. You're a great dad!" she reassured him and touched his hand.

"When your mom got pregnant with you, Delilah, she was a lot older than you are. She and I honestly thought we could not have children. I panicked at the thought of a baby. And you know that if you have a baby later in life, there is always the chance of the baby being born with disabilities.

We've talked about all of that. What you don't know is that I left your mom before you were born and did not come back into your lives until the day after your first birthday. I was a stupid, selfish man. And I was a coward."

Delilah sat there in total shock. She had never heard this story before. *The dad I know would never leave me.* She knew that if she could have seen him, she would have seen an old man with regret written all over his face.

"Daddy, you love me, right?"

"Oh, God, with every fiber in my body. I was foolish and scared. But I've tried so hard to make up for what I did."

She moved closer to him and whispered, "Did Mom forgive you?"

He looked at her with tears streaming down his face. "Yes, she did."

"Then I forgive you, too, Daddy," she said and laid her head on his shoulder.

Lifting her head, Delilah smiled and said, "Hey, Pop, you're going to be a grandpa!"

Adam grabbed his daughter and gave her a warm hug. She could tell that this had been something important that needed to be resolved and then put away. Forgiveness is a powerful thing.

The day came to hire a nanny. What a chore that turned out to be! Delilah was much more willing to bend than Adam and Daniel were. You would think this nanny had to speak five languages, be an armed guard, and manage to be a full chef. By the tenth nanny interview, Delilah had almost given up hope when in walked Brenda.

Brenda had a smooth Southern drawl. She was sophisticated, but most of all, she oozed kindness. She admitted to having been a single mom and to having raised her young son alone. She expressed hope that this would not sway their decision. Her son was in school full-time. She said that she hoped to work for a family that would also embrace her as family. Delilah touched Daniel's hand, and he knew she wanted this beautiful person in their home. Their job had been accomplished: Brenda, from the Blue Ridge Mountains of North Carolina, became their first nanny.

The months passed quickly. With Brenda's tender loving care, Delilah felt more confident each day about becoming a mother. Brenda taught her how to take care of a baby by using a doll. They carefully arranged the nursery so that Delilah would know where everything was. Delilah's goal was to be able to care for her baby with minimal assistance. Of course, she had Daniel, but Daniel still had to work. Delilah needed to be as self-sufficient as possible.

The pregnancy progressed without any problems. The closer it got to the birth, the more excited Daniel and Delilah became. Not everyone was as accepting of the upcoming birth. There was one day in particular when Delilah went for her OB-GYN appointment. Brenda had accompanied her because Daniel had to be away on business. She was about seven months along at the time and was obviously pregnant. Brenda escorted her into the clinic.

Brenda and Delilah were sitting in the waiting room when a pregnant woman—no, not a woman, a witch, according to Delilah—with a child leaned over to Brenda and whispered, "That is such a shame. Why in the world would a blind girl have a baby?"

Delilah perked up, looked toward the wretched voice, and said, "I am blind but no longer deaf. Why in the world would someone with such an ugly heart have a baby?"

Brenda could be heard giggling aloud.

The woman didn't say another word. She didn't know Delilah, and she messed with the wrong blind girl.

"Daniel!" Delilah screamed while holding her belly. "My water has broken. I think the baby is coming!"

She had been having contractions all day, but they were still pretty far apart. Brenda hadn't wanted to go home. Perhaps it was a premonition. Delilah told her to go pick up her son and to spend the night.

"Go get Brenda, Daniel. I need her!"

Just as Daniel wheeled out the door, Brenda was running down the hall.

"The baby is coming," Daniel said nervously.

"Okay, Daniel. Let Adam know. He may not have heard the commotion," said Brenda, who had gladly taken charge.

Adam ran down the stairs when he heard Daniel at the

bottom of the stairs yelling his name.

"Hi, Grandpa," said Delilah. "We're having a baby!"

"I, uh … I can see that, sweetheart," said Adam, stuttering while offering a squeamish smile.

Daniel wheeled close to Delilah and touched her arm. "Okay, baby, let's do this. Are you okay?"

Adam brought the van around, and Daniel wheeled his chair up the ramp and got into the driver's seat. Adam assisted Brenda in getting Delilah into the van. Just as they were seated, Delilah let out a piercing scream as she had another hard contraction.

Within minutes, they were taking Delilah into the delivery room at the hospital. The doctor said she was dilated to nine centimeters and would deliver soon. Daniel and Delilah had decided to be surprised as to whether it was a girl or a boy.

Adam called Mrs. Hamilton, Ms. Simms, Eddie and Beth, and Ben and Mia. Then he paced the floor. Daniel put on scrubs and was by Delilah's side. "I love you, Delilah!" said Daniel as he stroked her moist brow.

"I love you too, Daniel!"

With a couple of hard contractions and pushes, their new baby was born. Hearing the cries of the baby brought tears to Delilah's and Daniel's eyes.

"Congratulations, you have a son!" exclaimed the doctor, holding up a beautiful, perfect baby boy.

The nurse cleaned the baby and made the necessary

assessments. He weighed in at six pounds, four ounces.

When the nurse placed him in Delilah's arms, she could feel his soft skin and hear his sweet newborn sounds.

"Delilah, he is beautiful. He is very pink. He has black hair, long fingers, and little toes," explained Daniel.

"Oh, Daniel, I wish I could see him!"

"I know, honey, but you can feel him. You will be a great mother," responded Daniel, as he tried to console any feelings of sadness that Delilah may have felt. "Remember, you felt him move in your womb. You couldn't see him, but you felt him. You loved him, and you never saw him. He has already made his way into your heart. You will continue on the same journey."

Delilah gently touched her son's hair, smiled, and said, "You are so right, Daniel. I love him with my whole heart."

Daniel and Adam sat back as they watched Delilah holding her newborn son. They both agreed there was not a more beautiful sight than when Delilah smiles.

About the Author

Sunnie Day

Sunnie Day was raised in the military and has spent most of her adult life associated with military life, traveling to many places stateside and overseas. She enrolled in nursing school rather late in life and retired in 2011 after an eighteen-year nursing career. Since then, Sunnie has been able to resurrect her great love of writing.

Sunnie comments, "The time since my retirement has been a whirlwind as I began putting pen to paper. The words have flowed like a fast moving river, bringing with them many new adventures I never dreamed possible. My greatest hope is that my writing inspires and encourages others."

Sunnie raised four beautiful children who have now graced her with four wonderful grandchildren. She lives with her husband in central Texas.